THE WOT.

Further Titles by Leo Kessler from Severn House

The S.S. Wotan Series

ASSAULT ON BAGHDAD
BREAKOUT FROM STALINGRAD
FLIGHT FROM BERLIN
FLIGHT FROM MOSCOW
FIRE OVER SERBIA
OPERATION LONG JUMP
S. S. ATTACKS
THE WOTAN MISSION

THE HITLER WEREWOLF MURDERS

Writing as Duncan Harding

ATTACK NEW YORK!
COME HELL OR HIGH WATER!
OPERATION JUDGEMENT
OPERATION STORMWIND
THE TOBRUK RESCUE

Writing as Charles Whiting

The Common Smith VC Series

THE BALTIC RUN
DEATH ON THE RHINE
IN TURKISH WATERS
THE JAPANESE PRINCESS
PASSAGE TO PETROGRAD

PATHS OF DEATH AND GLORY
(*non-fiction*)

Writing as John Kerrigan

The O'Sullivans of the SAS Series

KILL ROMMEL

THE WOTAN MISSION

Leo Kessler

This first world edition published in Great Britain 1996 by
SEVERN HOUSE PUBLISHERS LTD of
9–15 High Street, Sutton, Surrey SM1 1DF.
First published in the USA 1996 by
SEVERN HOUSE PUBLISHERS INC of
595 Madison Avenue, New York, NY 10022.

Copyright © 1996 by Leo Kessler
All rights reserved. The moral rights of the author to be identified as author of this work have been asserted by him in accordance with the Copyright Designs and Patents Act 1988.

British Library Cataloguing in Publication Data
Kessler, Leo
  Wotan Mission. – (Wotan Series)
  I. Title II. Series
  823.914 [F]

ISBN 0-7278-4901-8

Typeset by Hewer Text Composition Services, Edinburgh.
Printed and bound in Great Britain by
Hartnolls Ltd, Bodmin, Cornwall.

PRELUDE TO A MISSION

"*Beide Motoren langsam voraus*," *Leutnant* Dreyer said in a subdued voice, as if he were afraid that the enemy was already listening to him.

At his side on the bridge of the huge Japanese submarine, Captain Yatamoto, squat and slant-eyed, repeated the order in Japanese. His voice was also low and careful, for he knew that after a voyage right round the world from Japan, they were now approaching the most dangerous part of their mission.

Slowly the *I 52* slid through the morning mist heading for the French coast, while on the slippery wet deck, the gun crews stood by, anxiously searching the grey sky for the first sight of the enemy, who they knew was there somewhere.

Without taking his gaze off his front for a moment, the young German officer explained the drill to the Japanese submarine commander. "In the old days when we still ran submarines from Lorient, we also entered or sailed at night. That was to prevent any agents that the enemy might have had among the local French population from reporting on our movements. Now we hope that by entering Lorient harbour at this time of the day, we might fool the *Amis* – Americans," the young blond officer added hastily, when he saw the Japanese captain didn't understand the word. "You see they're just over there." He pointed to the faint smudge of land to the east. "They've had the port of Lorient surrounded for three months nearly now."

The Japanese officer nodded his understanding and stared at the American-held land with a worried look in his slant eyes.

His explanation finished, Dreyer raised his binoculars once more and focused on the entrance to the estuary. According to the plan, the channel should have been swept during the night. Now he looked over the grey surface of the water to check whether the minesweepers had completed their task thoroughly. At his side the Japanese skipper waited anxiously for his verdict.

Dreyer lowered his glasses and said, "Looks all right, Captain." Then raising his voice a little, added, "Please tell the conning tower lookouts to keep their eyes skinned port and starboard."

The Japanese officer translated his words and the two lookouts trained their glasses on the channel, straining to spot any mine which might have been overlooked.

The minutes ticked by leadenly. A white-jacketed orderly brought up cups of bitter black coffee laced with saki. The two officers accepted them gratefully, as the orderly bowed and then clattered down the ladder back into the hull. "Nigger sweat," Dreyer said and took a gulp, "that's what we call it, Captain."

Yamamoto didn't respond. He was too anxious. He knew if he lost the second largest submarine in the Imperial Navy and was still alive afterwards, he would be forced to commit hara-kiri; his disgrace would be too great. So he kept his gaze focused on the white topped waves, occasionally turning to look up at the grey dawn sky.

Now, the squat outline of the great submarine pens

4

at Lorient, started to loom up. Dreyer nodded his approval. Once they were inside them there was nothing the *Amis* could do. For years now the Anglo-American air gangsters had been trying to knock them out, but without success. For a moment he allowed himself to dwell on what would happen this evening once they had berthed and reported. In spite of the month-long siege there was still plenty of drink and available women in Lorient.

After a long, satisfying bath, he would shave off his beard, put on a clean uniform, pin on the new medal they would have given him – everyone got a medal after a successful cruise and there weren't many successful ones these days – and go to the orgy.

He'd get drunk, then he'd take one of the French whores back to his quarters for the next twenty-four hours. Last time he had taken two with him and they had performed all those delightful little tricks on him, which made French whores so good in bed.

He smiled faintly at the thought. Two of them naked and playing games with each other as he watched, glass of champagne in one hand and a fat cigar in the other. Yes, he had lived as they said in Germany, "like the king in France".

Suddenly the vision of that bedroom scene vanished. An icy finger of fear traced its way down his spine. At the bow there was that insidious metallic scraping sound which he had dreaded ever since they had entered the channel. "*Stop both – at once!*"

The Japanese captain repeated the order in his own language and the big sub glided to a stop, as the Japanese looked at the young German as if he had suddenly gone mad. "What is it?" he demanded.

"A mine," Dreyer heard himself say in a voice he hardly

recognized as his own. He cocked his head to one side and listened hard, as his heart beat like a trip hammer. Next to him the three Japanese tensed. They knew what was at stake.

For what seemed an eternity nothing happened. Dreyer's breathing started to become normal again. Perhaps the damned thing had floated away. Then there it was again. That frightening rubbing of metal against metal. Sweat started to pour down his tense young face as he tried to spot it.

But it was the Japanese captain who saw the mine first. He grabbed Dreyer's arm and pointed. Together they stared in horrified fascination at the great black ball of steel, packed with high explosive, bobbing up and down just off the submarine's port bow. Twice those evil horns, that covered its dripping surface, almost touched the craft's hull; and twice a tiny wavelet washed the mine away in the last second.

Now the Japanese officer acted. He yelled something down the speaking tube. Two brawny petty officers, appeared as if by magic and lowered themselves to the slippery wet deck.

Dreyer swallowed painfully, as they tried to balance themselves on the hull, boathooks at the ready. Next to him the Japanese skipper gripped the casing in white-knuckled tension. Both men knew that if the petty officers made just one slip and hit these deadly prongs with their boathooks they'd be dead in an instant.

The bigger of the two petty officers nodded to the other one. Slowly, very slowly, he started to wedge his boathook between the horns, sweating furiously, as he tried to avoid the death-dealing mechanism.

Dreyer heard his heart beating madly in his ears. *Would they be able to pull it off?*

A minute later he had completed his task. The mine was now firmly wedged about half a metre from the hull of the submarine. Now the other one took over. He placed his clumsy boathook against the mine and together they prepared for the next step in this lethal game.

Now there was no sound, save that of the men's heavy breathing and the faint hiss of the spume from the sea. For what seemed an age the two petty officers poised there, holding the mine at a distance, knowing that if they relaxed their vigilance for one moment disaster would follow.

The bigger of the two nodded to his mate. The other responded with another nod. Dreyer could see their muscles flex through the thin material of their singlets. Together they bent on their poles. The mine moved!

Dreyer held his breath. Now they would attempt to walk it the length of the boat. Somehow the mine's cable had been severed. But if there was another obstruction anywhere while they walked it the length of the hull . . . Dreyer did not dare to think that particular thought.

Millimetre by millimetre the two Japanese started to ferry the mine the length of the casing, their breath coming in harsh audible gasps, as if they were running a great race, though in this case, it was with Death.

Then the mine was behind them bobbing up and down in the open channel. Dreyer wasted no more time. "Both ahead," he ordered, trying to control the note of near hysteria in his voice.

Hastily the Japanese skipper translated the order and the sub started to move forward once more, the loose mine disappearing in her white churning wake.

"Time's running out," Dreyer snapped, as the great sub pens at Lorient began to loom up larger and larger. "The Americans had observation posts on both sides of the channel. They will have picked us up on their radar by now, I should have thought."

The Japanese, face impassive, nodded his understanding and asked, "Can we take her up to ten knots?"

"Yes," Dreyer agreed quickly, as two kilometres away to the east a red light winked on the horizon. A moment later there was a great rushing sound like a huge piece of canvas being torn by giant hands. A dozen metres away the water erupted in a white fury and metal hissed lethally through the air. "A shell, they're on to us, the *Scheisshunde*! It won't be long now before they start to scramble their planes." He stared at the entrance to the bomb-proof pens with a look of longing in his bloodshot eyes.

But already the garrison at Lorient was taking up the challenge. Although shells were strictly rationed in the besieged port, those who knew about this top secret mission realized it was vital to provide the Japanese submarine with some protection. To the rear of the pens, the 88mm cannon burst into angry life. Almost immediately, great mushrooms of smoke started to rise on the American-held land spit.

"Holy strawsack!" Dreyer exclaimed with delight as the Germans guns thundered and the American shells started to land wide of the submarine because the Americans were rattled. "We're going to do it, Captain!"

The Japanese, a stoic man, returned his smile. "I think so," he answered in his accented German. He stopped short. "*Catalina*!" he shouted above the roar of the artillery.

"What?"

"American Catalina flying boat – to port. I see them often in Pacific. There."

Dreyer swung round. About a kilometre away, a

ugly-looking single-winged flying boat was heading their way slowly. Dreyer laughed contemptuously, as he heard the first strains of the march being played by the naval band, drawn up on the side of the great echoing pen to welcome.

"Too late! The *Amis* are too late!" he exclaimed. "They won't catch up with us now. We're home and dry."

A moment later the pen had swallowed them up in its massive concrete maws. And in the flying boat, an excited eighteen-year old US naval observer, clicking away with his camera as fast as he could, was crying excitedly. "*Gee wilikers, skipper . . . what in Sam Hill is a Jap sub doing in this neck of the wood . . .?*"

Part One

INTO THE HIGH VOSGES

Chapter One

Sergeant Schulze raised his massive right haunch and let rip one of those not unmusical farts for which he was justifiable celebrated throughout the whole of the SS NCO corps. "All right, you bunch of aspagarus Tarzans," he announced a little wearily, "you can put down yer curly little heads and snooze. We're home with mother and good decent Sergeant Schulze will look after yer."

At his side, his one-legged running mate Corporal Matz sniggered and said, "*Good decent* Sergeant Schulze – that'll be the frigging day!" He, too, let rip a great fart.

Schulze frowned down at him, taking in his ragged, battle-stained uniform, and told himself that Matz looked all-in, like the rest of the survivors of SS Assault Regiment Wotan did. They had been on the run for a month now, ever since their defeat in France in August. For four solid weeks they had retreated and fought, fought and retreated and now they were here in Alsace with not a single vehicle left from what had once been the most powerful Panzer regiment in the whole of the *Waffen SS*. No wonder his 'aspagarus Tarzans' looked so beat. Aloud he snorted, "None o' that undisciplined breaking of wind in public, Corporal Matz. Remember you are in the presence of a superior officer."

Matz looked up at his old running mate and raised what

he called his 'stinky finger'. "Piss in the wind, Schulze," he said. "Yer ain't got all yer cups in the cupboard if yer think there's any superior officers left. We're all in the same frigging boat with our hooters in the shit."

Watching the two old comrades, Colonel von Dodenburg, the commander of what was left of Wotan, grinned wearily and wiped the sweat off his brow with his tattered sleeve. Thank God for NCOs like the two of them, he told himself. Without them he wouldn't have got his survivors out of the mess this August of 1944. He raised his voice, and said, "Schulze . . . Matz, see if you can rustle up some fodder and drink for the men in the village." He looked at the little village street with the neat half-timbered Alsatian houses grouped round the onion-towered church. "They say that these Alsatians still live well – and after all they have been German citizens since 1940."

"Lot of frigging booty Germans!" Schulze exclaimed grumpily, and then added, "We'll see the laddies get some fodder and suds, as well, if there's any about."

Von Dodenburg nodded his approval. "I know you will, you big rogue. Off you go then. And there's an inn at the corner."

"Nuff said, sir," Schulze said. "I'm reading you loud and clear." He hitched his Schmeisser over his massive shoulder and snapped to Matz, "All right, you arse-with-ears, what yer waiting for?"

"Kiss my fart!" the other man said but he went willingly enough.

For a moment von Dodenburg watched the two of them heading straight for the little village inn, then he dismissed them from his mind, and turning stared at the high Vosges mountains to their rear.

Faintly now he could hear the rumble of heavy artillery

and a long way off he could just make out a tiny plane darting up and down over the peaks. That would be an American artillery spotter plane, he told himself. But it looked as if the American advance had been held up for a while. Now it was urgent for the defeated German Army in France to retreat to the safety of the great fortified *West Wall* which ran the length of the Reich's frontier with France and Belgium. There the survivors might be able to hold the advancing Allies.

He looked back at his men lying dirty, ragged and unshaven in the gutter of the village street and wondered if that would be possible. His men were the elite of the SS, but the only weapons they possessed were their machine pistols and rifles. What could they do against the massed American armour?

Von Dodenburg's harshly handsome face, pared down to the bone by the events of the last month, hardened. He no longer had any illusions about Hitler's vaunted '1,000 Year Reich'. The State was corrupt and run by a madman who had no idea of the real situation at the front. All the same he had his tribal loyalty to SS Wotan.

Now his primary duty was to save those weary young men as a tribute to all those other young men who had followed him so loyally to their deaths in Normandy. Mind made up, new purpose in his lean bronzed face Kuno von Dodenburg set off to find the local post office. If it possessed a telephone, which it should, he would get through to the nearest army official headquarters and ask for instructions.

Two hundred metres away, Schulze peered gingerly into the long limbered hall which led into the inn, 'the Hunter's Lodge'. Instinctively his nostrils twitched with delight as they caught the smell of stale beer and the sour whiff of *sauerkraut*. "We've landed in the gravy, old house," he whispered to Matz. "Fodder and suds. I can smell 'em with me hooter."

Matz nodded eagerly. "Me, too. Look me chin water's drooling down my kisser." He licked his lips in anticipation. "Come on, let's get to that lovely grub."

They hesitated no longer, but pushed deeper into the darkened hall of the inn, the floorboards creaking under their weight. Still, as eager as he was, Schulze kept his finger on the trigger of his Schmeisser. Over the last month they had had trouble enough with the *Maquis*, the French partisans, and he didn't really trust the Alsatians. Now that Germany was losing they might well have gone over to their former masters, the French.

Suddenly Schulze felt a draught of cooler air on his right cheek. Expert soldier that he was, Schulze swung round surprisingly quickly for such a huge man. A door had been opened somewhere, he knew that instinctively. "Out or I'll shoot!" he ordered grimly, Schmeisser tucked tightly to his hip.

"*Sch on gut, ich komme*," a female voice responded in accented Alsatian German. Next instant a hefty blonde, her breasts bursting through the tight silk material of her blouse, a short black skirt barely covering her ample thighs, came into view clutching a butcher's cleaver in her hand nervously.

"Heaven, arse and cloud exclaimed in amazement at the sights. "All that meat and no potatoes!"

Schulze licked his lips and growled, "Watch yer language in front of my fiancée." He looked at those massive breasts shimmering like huge melons under the tight blouse and reminded himself that it was a month since he had last done a woman the pleasure of handling his 'stiff German salami', as he always phrased it.

"You won't rape me?" the big woman said and lowered

the hatchet. There didn't seem to be much fear in her voice, Matz thought.

Schulze gave a courteous bow and said formally, "My beloved you'll be as safe with me, as if you were in a nunnery."

Matz sniggered and muttered, "That'll be the day." Then his stomach rumbled noisily and he said, "Gracious Miss, do you think you might find some poor vittels for two down-at-heel stubble hoppers who ain't scoffed no grub for a month?"

Ten minutes later the two of them were wolfing down a huge farmer's breakfast* straight from the frying pan in the kitchen, washing the hot food down with a litre glass of Mutzig Pils, while she stood there watching them with her brawny arms folded across that massive chest. Her fat face bore a look of anxious anticipation, as if she could not wait for them to be finished with the food . . .

A hundred metres away, the frightened little postal clerk, who kept insisting that "this is quite contrary to regulations, *Obersturmbannführer*," had finally connected von Dodenburg with army main headquarters in the Alsatian capital of Strasbourg.

"Wotan!" the Staff officer at the other end gasped when he reported. "We thought you had disappeared altogether. Thank God, you haven't! Please report your strength. Don't worry. The line is secure."

Von Dodenburg laughed grimly while the little wrinkled clerk tut-tutted, as if he were wondering that he might lose his precious pension for having allowed this call. "Strength, *Herr General*? Perhaps a hundred effectives with two NCOs and me."

---

* Fried potatoes, covered with scrambled egg and bacon. *Transl.*

The gasp at the other end was quite audible. "*Vehicles*? Every armoured vehicle is precious at this moment of crisis, von Dodenburg."

"None," von Dodenburg said harshly, annoyed a little at the staff officer's lack of understanding at what had happened in France. "We walked all the way back. Some of my men don't even have their dice-beakers," he meant their jackboots, "left. They're walking in their bare feet."

For a moment there was silence at the other end, then the General said, "You are to stay where you are for the moment, von Dodenburg. I have been told this very minute that Reichsführer SS Himmler will call personally within the hour to give you his orders. Is that understood?"

"Understood," von Dodenburg replied. The phone went dead.

"Did I hear the name Himmler?" the little civilian quavered.

"You did," von Dodenburg answered, his mind racing and elsewhere.

The man crossed himself . . .

Half an hour later, the phone shrilled urgently once more. The little civilian who wouldn't leave his office, despite the fact that other locals were beginning to flood the street to stare curiously at the ragged exhausted soldiers, now that they knew that the SS had come to their remote village with no intention of harming them, picked it up immediately. "*Poststelle Immerich*," he barked, standing to attention. "*Sie wunschen?*"

Next moment he swallowed hard, his prominent Adam's apple travelling up and down his skinny wrinkled neck like an express lift. "*Jawohl, Reichsführer, jawohl.*" He handed the phone to von Dodenburg as if it were red hot and burning his finger. "It's *Reichsführer* Himmler!" he exclaimed. Next moment he fled.

Chapter Two

Himmler chuckled with delight as he laid down the phone. Outside on Berlin's *Ost-West Allee* a shotdown American Flying Fortress was skidding down the great road, shredding bits of metal, trailing a fierce blowtorch of flame behind it, as it raced to its doom.

Standartenführer Zander, standing next to a gleeful Himmler's desk, raised his eye patch to get a better view of the dying US bomber, though he wasn't particularly interested in its fate. One had already been shot down, he reasoned, but there would be thousands more following. Day in, day out, they came and bombed, together with the Tommies at night, so that the German capital was now simply one great ruined shell.

Zander looked around as Himmler clapped his weak little hands in delight, chortling, "Now we're showing those *Ami* swine!" On the other side of the debris-littered road, two elderly Red Cross men were bearing out a dying zebra on a stretcher. Next to them, a wounded monkey from the same zoo hobbled along on one leg. None of them paid any attention to the dead woman sprawled in the gutter, her skirt thrown up and her legs spread in one last obscene invitation.

Zander shook his head and lowered the black eye patch. He had seen enough. Germany had gone completely crazy. That little scene seemed to exemplify that.

At the end of the *Allee*, the crippled Flying Fortress crashed into a stationary fire engine and exploded in one great deafening roar that seemed to go on for ever. "Great crap on the Christmas tree!" Zander cursed to himself, "What a frigging world!"

Himmler clapped his hands with sheer delight. His dark eyes sparkled behind the prissy, gold-rimmed pince-nez he affected, which made him look like some high school teacher instead of the most feared man in Occupied Europe which he was. "Ah," he exclaimed, "so there goes another of those perverted air gangster of theirs. If I had my way I'd string up any of them that we capture from the nearest lamppost." He shrugged. But you know the Führer, Zander. He is simply just too kind-hearted. He cleared his throat and the thin smile of triumph on his sallow weak-chinned face vanished. "I have just spoken to von Dodenburg of Wotan. You know him, Zander?"

Zander pointed to his eye patch, his tough craggy face breaking into a grin. "*Jawohl, Reichsführer*. He helped me to get this in Kursk in '43. Brave bastard, if you'll forgive me, and decidedly arrogant. Doesn't like taking orders."

Himmler obviously did not quite understand how to take Zander's answer so he rasped, "Well, he'll take orders from *me, Standartenführer*."

The other man was unimpressed by Himmler's threatening manner. What more could be done to me, he asked himself. He was virtually blind in one eye, his left arm had gone and his balls had almost been shot away. No, *Standartenführer* Zander reasoned, nothing really could frighten him any more. Besides when the Russians came and if he was still in Berlin, they'd line him up against the nearest wall within five minutes and shoot him. That would be the fate of all the SS officers they captured. "Where's the fire then, *Reichsführer?*" he asked.

Himmler looked nervously from side to side as if he were afraid of being overheard and answered, "Zander, I'm going to entrust you with one of the greatest secrets of this war."

Zander waited, his craggy face revealing nothing, save perhaps cynical boredom.

"Our scientists, Zander, having lost most of their facilities through the enemy terror bombing, can no longer work on this project. But since 1941 they had been trying to perfect what they called the atomic bomb and have achieved a great deal of success."

Zander showed some interest. Outside the sirens were beginning to shrill the 'all clear'. "Atomic bomb, what's that, *Reichsführer?*"

"A bomb more powerful than any hitherto known. The scientists maintain one bomb could destroy a whole city. Think, what a war-winning weapon that would be."

Zander whistled softly. Now he was impressed.

Himmler's look of happiness vanished at the thought that Germany wouldn't be able to destroy whole cities just yet; that would have to be left to Germany's ally now. "So," he continued, "the Führer has decided in his wisdom that the secret will be given to our ally Japan, who will continue the research. And here there is a mission for you and von Dodenburg's Wotan, what is left of it—"

"Excuse me, *Reichsführer,*" Zander butted in with that straightforward approach of his, which had always made him unpopular with pompous, long-winded superior officers. "Why Japan?"

"Because, my deary fellow," Himmler said heartily, "we are going to continue the war even if we are defeated here in the Reich."

"How do you mean, *Reichsführer?*"

"If the Third Reich has to die, then we shall create a Fourth Reich, which will carry on our holy National Socialist cause until the time comes to reconquer old homeland. For that we need the Japanese and the atomic bomb. For take it from me, Zander, *they* will never surrender."

Zander, for the first time, looked a little bewildered and Himmler enjoyed the look on that craggy, tough face opposite him. He said, "*Nun, mein lieber Herr*, you are obviously wondering where that Fourth Reich might be set up, until we can march back into Europe with the aid of our Japanese bomb." He chuckled. "I shall tell you. South America!"

Outside a woman who had gone mad in the bombing was screeching at the top of her voice. "*Fuck God . . . Damnwell fuck God . . . He shouldn't allow this to happen . . . Fuck God, people—*" A single shot rang out and the screaming ended abruptly. Obviously one of the special police on the streets after an air raid had shot the hysterical woman before she spread the panic.

Zander pulled a face and said, "But how can we do that, *Reichsführer?*"

Himmler made the continental gesture with his forefinger and thumb of counting banknotes. "That way. We can buy most of those tinpot South American dictators. We've already had discussions with some of them. Never fear, my dear fellow, as long as we have gold and diamonds and the Japs are prepared to help us, we can establish the Fourth Reich without too much difficulty. But to set the ball rolling, we need brave fellows like you and young Kuno von Dodenburg. You will be our couriers of hope, the heralds of a new future for our beloved Germany—"

He stopped short as the light above the door started to flash on and off in a bright red. "Ah, ah," Himmler said, "*Herr Bankdirektor* Grimm of the Reichsbank. As punctual as a bricklayer as they used to say when I was a boy in Munich." He pressed the button on his desk.

Immediately the door was opened by a gigantic adjutant in the black uniform of the pre-war SS, machine pistol, slung across his massive chest, helmet gleaming as if it had been just polished. He clicked to attention and yelled at the top of his voice, "*Herr Bankdirektor* Grimm! *Reichsführer*." His right arm shot out and he followed the announcement with, "Heil Hitler", shouting the words as if he were back at the SS Cadet School at Bad Toelz.

"*Danke, Schmidt. Reintreten lassen.*"

The adjutant stepped to one side woodenly and again shouted, "*Der Reichsfuhrer SS laesst bitten.*"

There was a moment's pause, then a small grey man entered the room, dressed in black jacket and striped pants, with the party badge prominently displayed on his right lapel. He clicked his heels stiffly together and gave an equally stiff bow. "*Generaldirektor* Grimm of the Reichsbank. I have the honour." He boxed again.

Typical civilian arse-with-ears, Zander told himself, an arsecrawler first class. One of those who for the last ten or eleven years had made a bundle out of the '1,000 Year Reich'. First they had made it out of the Jews who had had to flee Germany and then out of the occupied territories. What had they said in Russia? 'First the tanks and then the Dresdner Bank.'

"Good to see you, *Herr Direktor*," Himmler said. "Please take a seat. This is *Standartenführer* Zander, who will be part of the operation we have discussed."

Grimm gave Zander a tight, gold-toothed smile, his

mouth working, as if it were operated by stiff metal wires. The SS officer's dislike of the banker increased.

"Now then," Himmler said, as the giant adjutant closed the door behind. "Let us add some more details to this operation which I have now decided to call 'The Wotan Mission'. You'll learn why later."

Outside the sirens had begun to sound their shrill warning once more. Grimm paled, his furtive ratlike eyes suddenly full of fear. The *Amis* were on their way back for yet another daylight raid.

Himmler tried to ignore the danger now approaching Berlin once more. He flashed one nervous look through the bulletproof window of his office and said hastily, "Just in case we have to go to the shelters, let me say this now. Grimm, you are in charge of the financial side of this operation. You will supply the diamonds and the foreign currency needed. Make sure that the notes are in large denominations. The less bulk you have to transport the better. You, Zander, are overall commander." He looked pointedly at the SS General. "On pain of death you take full and absolute responsibility for the other matter I have already spoken about."

Zander nodded. Himmler obviously meant this new-fangled atomic bomb material he had just mentioned.

"The task force you will use, will be made up of von Dodenburg's Wotan. I shall see that they are rearmed and re-supplied this very day."

Now the window was rattling as the flak guns opened up and Zander could see the tracer zipping into the sky like glowing golf balls. But even the bark of the anti-aircraft guns could not hide the thunder of the massive force of US bombers rapidly approaching Berlin.

Grimm heard the noise and he started to tremble so badly that his teeth chattered. Zander looked at him contemptuously. The man was an absolute coward. Himmler had grown even paler, too. In the moment both of them would racing down the stairs to the bombproof shelter in the building's basement.

It was time, he told himself, to find out what his objective was, before the two of them picked up their heels and did a bunk. "One quick question, *Reichsführer?*" he yelled above the thunder of the bombers outside.

"Yes, Zander." Himmler had already stood up and reached for his cap with a hand that was trembling badly.

"Our objective, sir?" he yelled.

"Back to France!" Himmler yelled back and then he and Grimm were rushing for the door as the first of the new bombs came howling down. Zander stared after them open-mouthed like some village yokel. "Back to France?" he echoed dumbfounded. "Well, I'll go and piss in my boot." Next moment the blast threw him off his feet, his face still set in a look of absolute amazed bewilderment.

Chapter Three

The enemy Thunderbolt caught up with them just after they had crossed the Moselle. They were flying in a flight of three Fieseler Storchs with Zander's plane in the lead and Grimm's bringing up the rear. The middle one contained no passenger, for it contained the precious stones and the top secret material for the new and deadly bomb.

Now suddenly the radial-engine enemy fighter came huntling out of the sun in a silver streak at five hundred kilometres an hour, cannon chattering. "Holy strawsack." Zander's pilot yelled in alarm and automatically throttled back, so that the stream of white glowing cannon shells just missed them. "Now the fur and snot's going to fly!"

Zander didn't answer, as he seized the light plane's single machine gun and swung it round. Five hundred metres away, the Thunderbolt made a tight curve, trailing brown smoke behind it. Below, the other two Storchs had begun to hedge-hop, knowing that this was their best defence against the high speed American fighter.

"Here the prick comes again," the pilot yelled over the intercom, as the Thunderbolt's pilot lowered his undercarriage to slow the heavy fighter down, "and he knows his stuff."

Zander didn't reply. He was concentrating on the

fighter, growing larger by the second in the circle of the machine gun's ring sight. "This is going to be crap or bust," he said grimly to himself, and took aim.

Now the Thunderbolt was five hundred metres or less away. The Storch pilot let the light plane drop alarmingly, his prop wash whipping the foliage of the trees below back and forth in a crazy frenzy. Still the American pilot hung on to the plane. He was determined to knock the impudent little Storch out of the sky.

Zander tensed. The silver mass of the Thunderbolt seemed to fill the whole heavens. "*NOW!*" he yelled, feeling the adrenalin flood his veins in that old thrill when he hadn't cared whether he was going to live or die, carried away by that primeval urge of battle.

The Thunderbolt opened fire. Tracer zipped towards the Storch in a lethal morse in the same instant that Zander pressed his own trigger. Suddenly all was chaos, noise, the stink of burnt explosive. The final battle had commenced . . .

Down below, the street of the little Alsatian village was filled with Wotan troopers, shading their eyes against the slanting rays of the autumn sun, as they peered upwards at the uneven battle.

Mounted on his 'betrothed', as he called the huge Alsatian woman, who now lay spreadeagled, panting hard, body lathered in sweat, with her fat white legs round Schulze's shoulders, the latter risked a look through the window at the grim duel taking place in the sky. For a second, he missed a stroke and the 'betrothed' gasped, "Don't stop . . . oh please don't stop. *I'm coming!*"

"Yer, like frigging Christmas is coming!" Schulze muttered grumpily, for this was the fifth time he had given her a taste of his 'good German salami' this afternoon, and the strain was beginning to tell. Then he dismissed the aerial battle with, "Silly friggers shouldn't go up in aeroplanes in the first place. Frigging unnatural," and continued with his labour of love . . .

Suddenly Zander got lucky. The pilot of the Thunderbolt attempted a deflection burst, forgetting that he was flying at almost stalling speed. In an instant the big fighter almost went out of control. Hastily the pilot hit the throttle and the Thunderbolt overshot the Storch.

For one long second Zander had the full view of the fighter's solver belly. He could even make out the oil-stained rivets just beneath the radial engine. It was a chance not to be missed. Face hard and set, he cried, "Try this one on for size, you prick." Then he pressed the trigger.

Tracer zipped upwards. At that range Zander couldn't miss. Pieces of metal flew from beneath the Thunderbolt. For one moment it seemed to falter in midair, then it flew on, its engine giving off ominous spluttering sounds. For one minute Zander thought his burst had not been effective. Then suddenly, startlingly, the Thunderbolt went totally out of control. It fell from the sky like a silver hawk.

"*Himmel, Arsch und zugenaht!*" the pilot of the Storch cried in triumph as the Thunderbolt hit the ground. It slithered forward across the field, shedding bright silver metal all the while. Then it smashed into an ancient oak. Next instant it exploded in a great angry ball of scarlet flame.

On the bed, the big Alsatian woman cried in her ecstasy. "The earth moved, my darling . . . oh, the earth just moved!" She gave one final gasp and went limp, her hands trailing over the sides of the rumpled bed, as if she might be dead.

Schulze, gasping mightily, rolled off her and commented, "Ay, the frigging earth did move all right. *Phew!*"

As the first of the little planes started to land on the village's football ground, a square of bare earth just behind the onion-tower church, von Dodenburg nodded to Matz. "Just in case, Corporal Matz, whistle up a squad and keep me covered." He loosened the flap of his pistol holster.

Sore as he was that Schulze wouldn't let him share the charms of his 'betrothed' – "There's enough meat on that one for two of us, Schulze," he had protested in vain – Matz answered quickly enough. For like all the Wotan troopers he admired the C.O. intensely. He knew as they did, that von Dodenburg would never sacrifice his men for his own glory. "Will do, sir," he snapped, as the C.O. started to stride towards the first of the planes. He turned, cupped his hands round his mouth and yelled in the direction of the inn where Schulze was, "Get the digit out of the orifice, Schulze, yer needed down here. All right, you . . . you and you . . . follow me!"

Swiftly the little squad, machine pistols at the ready, started to follow von Dodenburg, as the first pilot turned off his engine and the canopy was thrown back.

Von Dodenburg halted in his tracks as he saw the officer wearing the stars of a brigadier general appear in the cockpit. He clicked to attention and flung up his right arm in the official salute. "*Heil*—" he began but was interrupted by Zander.

"Cut out that crap, Kuno. That's frigging ancient history now."

"*Standartenführer* Zander!" von Dodenburg exclaimed

in surprise. What was Zander doing in this remote hamlet?

"*Heinz,*" Zander corrected him as he dropped to ground. "Hell, in the old days we've drunk vodka out of each other's boot in Russia. None of this *Standartenführer* piss." He held out his one arm and a slightly dazed von Dodenburg took it, telling himself his old comrade of the battles in Russia had aged greatly since those days. He looked at least twenty years older than the thirty-five that he was.

Zander saw the look and said with a cynical smile, "Office life, Kuno. Makes a wreck of a man. Too much firewater and too many ready and willing secretaries who'll do just anything for a war hero." He tapped his chest covered with medals. He laughed and von Dodenburg did the same.

Zander grew serious. "Get a squad together to unload these planes toot sweet. I want the Storchs out of here in fifteen minutes. They attract too much attention and that is the last thing we need now."

Too busy to ask questions – and he had plenty of them – von Dodenburg organized the unloading of the planes and, together with the runt of a civilian, Grimm, who was obviously very frightened Zander and he walked back to the inn which was now his headquarters, those of the old hares who had known Zander in Russia snapping to attention and saying, "Welcome back to the front, sir . . . just like home it is."

Zander was obviously very pleased to be back to the 'stubble hoppers', as he called them, von Dodenburg could see that. More than once he stopped when he recognized a familiar face and a couple of times he patted the cheeks of the youngsters, saying, "Well done, sonny. You put up a good show in France. The Fatherland

31

won't forget it." Then he came up to Schulze, who had somehow had managed to slip into his uniform in time, though for some reason known only to himself, he was wearing a pair of red silk knickers on his shaven skull.

"*Schulze!*" he exclaimed. "You old horned ox! Thought you'd been croaked years ago." He stopped short and looked at the knickers. "But why in three devils' name are you wearing those silk drawers on yer turnip?"

Schulze didn't bat an eyelid, though he had forgotten that he was wearing his 'betrothed's' knickers. "With the General's permission, beg to report that my head wound is still bleeding. Do not wish to demoralize the younger men with the sight of my blood. Red knickers hide the blood. Hence female undergarments, *sir!*"

Zander looked at the big noncom open-mouthed for a moment before exploding, "What a load of bullshit, you rogue! I can see yer still up to yer old tricks." And with that he gave Schulze a punch in his right shoulder which sent even that giant staggering back.

But once inside the taproom of the little Alsatian inn, with Matz standing guard outside the door – "What a bunch of cripples the SS has become, you Matz, with yer leg sabred off, me with one flipper gone!" – Zander's mood became sombre, almost pensive. He sat with his back to the green tiled stove, which crackled merrily, sipping moodily at the fiery local Kirsch brandy before saying, "Von Dodenburg, the Reichsfuhrer has placed you and your brave fellows under my command. We've been given a special and highly important mission."

Von Dodenburg frowned and Zander said hastily, putting down his glass, "I know, I know, Kuno, your fellows are exhausted. They've had enough. I'm not blind. I can see that."

"A German soldier is never exhausted," Grimm, who was primly drinking soda water, pontificated.

"*Herr Direktor*," Zander said, "you might know something about money, but you don't know a *spitting* thing about what the ordinary stubble hopper goes through in the line. So please, *Herr Direktor*," he emphasized the title with a sneer, "keep your opinions to yourself, when front swine like ourselves are talking." Zander poured himself another drink. "All right, Kuno, I'll lay it on the line. We're going back into France."

Von Dodenburg whistled softly and looked hard at Zander's craggy face to see if he was being serious. But he obviously was.

"And that's not the end of it," Zander continued, taking a hefty slug of the brandy. "We're going in wearing American uniforms." With his one eye he looked keenly at the harshly handsome younger officer. "And you know what that means if we're taken alive."

"Yes," von Dodenburg answered without any dramatics, "we'll be shot out of hand, Heinz."

At von Dodenburg's side, Grimm shivered violently and almost dropped his glass of soda water.

Chapter Four

Camille, the French waiter who always served Commander Ian Fleming, R.N. at Frascati's Restaurant in London, beamed when he spotted his favourite client, following the somewhat portly head of Naval Intelligence, Admiral Godfrey, into the restaurant's Edwardian dining room. "Ah, good-day, gentlemens." He chortled, rubbing his soft hands together, as if in anticipation of the fat tip which Fleming always gave him. "I am having something special for you today, gentlemens." He lowered his voice so that the other diners couldn't hear. "Mushromps on toast and a nice bottle of white wine."

Fleming gave the waiter one of his sardonic smiles, which had always made Fleming very attractive to women of a certain age. "*Mushrooms*," he corrected.

"Yes, I am saying that, sir – mushromps."

"Oh give up, Ian," Godfrey said, and sat down in the largest chair at the table, "we know what he means. Better than dried egg and that damned South African snoek at least. Main thing there's a decent tipple." The Admiral lowered his voice, though the security was good in the dining room with the tables being well spread out. "Anything?"

Fleming opened the briefcase with its self-igniting device if anyone unauthorized attempted to open it.

"Yessir," he answered and passed over the large black and white photograph. "My little lady with the built-in foxhole, as the Yanks say, was very obliging."

Godfrey looked puzzled and then he got it. "I see – *built in foxhole*." God, aren't the Yanks coarse!" He accepted the photograph and stared at it, while Fleming lit one of the specially handmade cigarettes he obtained from his Bond Street tobacconist and placed it in his ivory cigarette holder.

He let the Admiral take his time, remembering the half an hour strenuous lovemaking with the rather plain American girl who had given him the photograph obtained from US Naval Intelligence. Still, plain as she was, she did that thing which he always associated with French women in bed.

"Jap I class, isn't it?" Godfrey concluded finally. "Biggest they've got."

"That's right, sir," Fleming concluded, his clean face with the nose that he had broken at Eton, revealing nothing. "They use them for long range fighting patrols, but they also use them," he lowered his voice to emphasize the point, "for carrying cargo."

Godfrey grunted, but said nothing. He knew just how deviously Fleming's mind worked. Sometimes the young commander came up with some absolutely idiotic schemes. More than once he had told Fleming, "Ian you ought to have been a damned thriller writer, the awful penny dreadful stuff you come up with." But Fleming had done some very useful work for Naval Intelligence ever since he had taken up his post in the famed Room 39 at the Admiralty. So he waited.

Fleming made him wait a little longer. Overhead a V-I was chugging across London, sounding like a battered two-stroke motorcycle, but no one took much notice.

They had been falling on the capital since June and everyone said, "There's nothing you can do about them. If they've got your number on 'em. That's that."

Finally Fleming broke his silence. "Will you be so kind as to look a little more closer at the background, in particular, to the left, sir," he said politely.

Godfrey was a vain man. He thought sailors should never be seen wearing spectacles, even if they were middle-aged. This time however, he pulled a reading glass from his breast pocket and peered at the photograph once again, noting that the Americans had marked it 'Top Secret'. He smiled faintly. How little did the Yanks realize that 'Top Secrets' meant very little to their women when Fleming bedded them, the rogue.

Outside the putt-putt of the V-I's engine had eased. In the restaurant people tensed, some with the spoons to their lips, others holding on to their glasses more tightly; they knew what was coming. There was a sudden crash. The place shook. Then a tall mushroom of black smoke started to ascend into the autumn sky to where the barrage balloons swayed back and forth like tethered elephants. The chatter and eating commenced at once.

Godfrey whistled and put down the photograph. "Sub pens!" he exclaimed. "The sub pens at Lorient on the French coast, if I'm not mistaken."

"You're not, sir. I had our expert go over it with a fine-tooth comb. They're the Lorient sub pens all right."

Godfrey looked puzzled. "But what would a Jap sub he doing there, Ian? As soon as the Yanks encircled the place in August, the *Kriegsmarine** withdrew all their U-boats. It was proving too difficult to get them in and out into the Atlantic."

* The German Navy. *Transl.*

"Exactly, sir," Fleming agreed smoothly. "All they've got there now are a few E-boats, used for running up and down the channel and taking on the Yanks. What supplies they get, they do by raiding the local countryside and what can be dropped to the garrison by air."

"So why the Jap?" Godfrey persisted in bewilderment.

"I think we can look at it two ways, sir," Fleming answered. "Either the Jap sub is there to bring something *in* or it's there to take it *out*. After all the I-Class are large-scale underwater cargo carriers."

"But it does seem a bit daft, Ian, to send a Jap sub half-way round the world to take something to a French port which is tightly besieged," Godfrey objected. "What purpose would that serve?"

"That is my thinking, sir."

"So the Japs are going to take something *out* for the Hun."

Fleming nodded and took his eyes off a woman in her forties with startling red hair who was smiling winningly at him and uncrossing and crossing her legs very carelessly to reveal that she wasn't a true red head after all. "Yes, I came to that conclusion, too, sir."

Godfrey smiled his admiration. "As the *Herrenvolk** say in their bloody language, Ian, you can hear the damned grass growing."

"Thank you, sir."

"But what in heaven's name can the Germans be wanting the Japs to transport for them, to wherever it can go?" Godfrey asked in some bewilderment.

"Well, sir, I've sounded several people in the know about that, sir." Fleming answered thoughtfully. "You

---

* Master race. *Transl.*

know the bar at White's is like an intelligence centre – and *do* the SIS people gossip."

"Lot of drunks. Old Menzies," he meant the head of the Secret Intelligence Centre who often held court at White's Club, "has picked a queer lot to work for him – pansies and boozers, the whole shower of 'em."

Patiently Fleming waited for his chief to finish his little outburst. He knew there was no love lost between Admiral Godfrey and General Menzies, the head of the rival intelligence service. Then when he had finished, Fleming said, "It seems from what I've heard, sir, that some Germans, *important* Germans, are trying to make provisions for what might happen after the Third Reich's defeat. Already they have tried to set up an undercover ring among the Hungarian nobility with those vast farms of theirs on the *puzta*, to carry on the Fascist cause once the Reich goes under. They've made soundings elsewhere – even in Southern Ireland, where they are supporting the IRA, as you know."

"Damned Micks." Godfrey snorted.

"They did it after the last war of course – in Sweden, Holland, even in Soviet Russia—"

"I know, I know, Ian," Godfrey interrupted him. "Get on with the present."

"Yessir," Fleming answered obediently. "Well last month, a group of German industrialists – they call themselves, the 'Friends of the Führer' – met in Strasbourg on the Franco-German border. We don't know all the details of that meeting, but all the Nazi bigshots were there, including the head of the Reichsbank and the Dresdner Bank for example."

"Go on."

"But one thing we have found out – or rather Menzies' boys have – is that there was a general agreement to ship

German assets, hard currency, gold bullion, diamonds and the like abroad. The aim naturally is to finance the future of the Nazi state abroad, once the Third Reich is defeated."

"But no one in his right mind is going to support a continuation of that Nazi abomination elsewhere especially in Europe, Ian. We wouldn't allow it." He looked severely at Fleming. "Is this another of your penny-dreadful ideas, Ian?"

"No sir," Fleming replied firmly. "There are umpteen banana republics, most of them Fascist, in South America, remote sort of places we know little about, which would be only too glad to accept Nazi money."

The Admiral considered for a few moments before saying, "I suppose you *could* be right, Ian. I did a cruise off South America with our squadron out there back in '35 and there were a lot of rum politicos about then. All right," his voice rose, "what are you proposing we should do about it?"

Fleming was ready with his answer. "This, sir. We've got an SBS team on the French coast in that area. Now—"

"SBS?" Godfrey broke in.

"*Special Boat Service*, mostly made up of Royal Marines. You know the chaps who go in and sabotage and the like off enemy coasts, formed back in '41 at the same time as the SAS?"

Godfrey nodded. "Now I remember. Carry on."

"Well, sir, they're linked up with the local French Maquis. I think they should be ordered to do a recce on this Jap sub and see what they can find out."

Godfrey nodded his head. "All right, it shall be done. But it's all very rum, very rum indeed." And then he dismissed the matter, as Camille appeared bearing on a silver tray his celebrated 'Mushromps on toast' and a bottle of chilled white wine.

But in later years he would always boast to anyone prepared to listen, "Shall I tell you how I stopped the Nips winning the war." But then there were few prepared to listen. After all World War Two had become a very boring subject.

Chapter Five

It was bitterly cold for September. At the forward observation post the Maquis sentry stamped his feet, his face burrowed in the collar of his British greatcoat. Ever so often he breathed out hard so that his warm breath circulated around the collar and warmed his ears temporarily. It would be another thirty minutes before his spell of guard duty was over, but already he was longing to warm himself in front of the pot-bellied stove in the Alsatian *Wirtshaus*, which the Maquis had taken over as their headquarters.

Behind him the little village slept. Now it was inhabited solely by the Maquis. All the Alsatian villagers, pro-Boche to the man, had been evacuated to the rear, where probably most of them were now languishing behind bars in one of De Gaulle's jails. It served them right, the skinny young sentry told himself. During the Occupation they had all kissed the Boche's arse for what they could get out of the enemy.

He shivered again. He would dearly have loved to have lit one of the fine ration American cigarettes the Americans gave them, but their American instructor had warned them never to smoke on sentry duty at night. It gave your position away. Instead he stared around at the shadows a little apprehensively, as a spectral moon scudded in and out of the clouds. Suddenly he wished he was back in his native Lyons instead of up here in these freezing German mountains. He stamped his feet and started to walk his beat again; that would pass the time until his relief.

He heard the slight noise when it was already too late. He turned, mouth open to cry out, fumbling with his slung rifle. Too late! A heavy, muscular arm crooked itself round his skinny neck. The cry was stifled. Noiselessly, expertly, the razor-sharp blade slid between his third and fourth rib. His body arched like a bow. Still he could not break that vicelike grip. The knife came out with an obscene sucking noise. Once more it thrust into his skinny frame. Slowly the Maquis sentry's legs began to buckle. Then he was dead. Carefully Corporal Matz lowered him to the frozen ground, sparkling icily in the cold harsh light of the moon.

He wiped his knife clean on the dead man's coat, rifled his pocket for cigarettes and when he found them, muttered to himself, "Better than the horseshit they give us to smoke", thrusting his blood-stained fingers into them. Like grey ghosts the rest of the Wotan troopers came stealing out of the shadows almost noiselessly.

Schulze looked down at the still figure on the frozen ground and whispered, "Poor shit!"

Matz shrugged, though he didn't like what he had just done. "You weren't saying that when the bastards were sniping and shooting our boys in the back, on the retreat through Frogland," he hissed.

"Suppose yer right," Schulze agreed.

Von Dodenburg and Zander, both dressed in captured US uniforms like the rest of the Wotan troopers, with only Grimm still dressed in his German civilian clothes, came up. They eyed the silent half-timbered houses to their front. From Intelligence they knew they were held by a small force of Maquis, with the main US line higher up the mountains.

"We'll try to do it without making too much noise," Zander said softly. "The main thing is to get those *Ami* trucks of theirs. We've got to have them if we're going to get through any American road block."

Von Dodenburg nodded his understanding and hissed, "*Los!*"

In a loose skirmish line the Wotan troopers moved forward, nerves tingling with suppressed tension. There was no sound as they crossed the frozen ground, save the drip-drip of a burst pipe in one of the medieval houses.

Von Dodenburg bent his head to avoid the shrivelled yellow tobacco leaves hanging from one of the low eaves of the first house. They had probably been left there by some Alsatian peasant who had been taken away when the Maquis had first entered the Vosges mountains. "Schulz, take Matz and a handful of the boys and secure the trucks before the balloon goes up."

"Will do, sir," Schulze answered dutifully and disappeared round the back of the house into the glowing, silver darkness.

Von Dodenburg poised at the door of the house and threw a glance at the green dial of his wrist-watch. He started to count off the seconds under his breath. At his side Zander turned and stared anxiously to the east where the German positions were. "*Now!*" von Dodenburg cried in the very same instant that the German multiple mortars a kilometre away burst into action to drown the Wotan attack.

To their rear, bombs exploded in burst of furious red flame, breaking the night silence instantly. Von

Dodenburg flew through the door. A half-dressed partisan, limp cigarette hanging from the corner of his mouth, was seated at the kitchen table, playing cards in the hissing white light of a petrol lantern. Four others snored open-mouthed on their bedrolls on the floor. Another hunched over an American radio receiver. He grabbed for the pistol lying on the table next to the radio.

Von Dodenburg didn't give him a chance to use it. His own pistol spat fire. The man shrieked and slumped over the radio, blood from his shattered upper arm jetting out in a bright scarlet arc.

Next to von Dodenburg, Zander, legs spread like a cowboy gunslinger in a Hollywood movies, pressed the trigger of his machine pistol, weaving from left to right.

Wood splintered. The man who had been playing *solitaire* stared at the line of red buttonholes stiched across his skinny chest in total disbelief. This couldn't be happening to him. Then he fell backwards overturning the wooden chair. On the floor the other four Maquis died as they slept. In a matter of minutes it was all over and the Wotan troopers were in command of the forward post in this remote hamlet in the Vosges Mountains.

Now as the mortar barrage ceased as abruptly as it had started, leaving behind it a loud echoing silence which reverberated in the circle of mountains, the SS troopers streamed through the houses, looting and wrecking as they went. No prisoners were taken on Zander's orders. "We can't spare any men to take them to rear – and we want no witnesses of our passing," he had declared firmly. "*Shoot 'em!*" And that had been that.

By midnight it was all over. The defenders of the village outpost were all dead and the troopers were happily stuffing their pockets and haversacks with delicacies of a kind they hadn't seen for years. Schulze and Matz, as always, had been successful in locating the only firewater in the village – two bottles of fruit schnaps – *Quetsch*. Now Schulze raised his bottle happily, big thick American cigar tucked behind his right ear, and cried, "Stand by tonsils, you're gonna get a treat!" With that he poured a hefty slung down his greedy throat.

A few metres away, the two SS officer and the civilian, Grimm, conferred in the silver darkness, staring at the high Vosges as they did so. "All we know," Zander concluded, "is that immediate positions below the peaks are held by American Nisei. And if they take after their Japanese forefathers they're going to be a tough nut to crack. So we shall try to avoid them till we're down in the valleys beyond."

"*Nisei*?" Grimm queried puzzled.

"Yes, Japanese-Americans. For some strange reason, although the Amis have interred most of their people back in the United States, three thousand of them or more, volunteered to fight in Europe. We first met them in Italy. Now they're here in France."

"Curious," Grimm said.

"It's a funny old world," Zander said and gave a cynical laugh. "What about those renegade German generals captured at Stalingrad now fighting for the Ivans." He meant the Russians. "But no matter. Let's get on with this business."

Von Dodenburg nodded his agreement. "Before those two rogues," he indicated Matz and Schulze drinking in the moonlight, "get too drunk."

"Well, we'll take the *Route des Crestes*," Zander continued. "It runs across the top of the mountains. The French built it secretly during the First World War when there was a lot of fighting up here in the Vosges.

It's pretty steep, but those *Ami* trucks will be able to make it. But it would be no good for heavily laden supply trucks. So our Intelligence reasons there will be little *Ami* supply traffic using it. I hope they're right." He turned to Grimm. "You can supervise the loading of your stuff. I, personally, will take care of *Reichsführer* Himmler's things. Come on. There's no time to be wasted."

He strode, away, not waiting for Grimm, while van Dodenburg watched him depart, his face puzzled. Zander was usually a pretty outspoken officer. Why was he being so mysterious about the crate and what appeared to be a briefcase stuffed with documents of some kind? What great secret could he be keeping to himself? Then he dismissed the matter and started to carry out his own duties.

"All right, you couple of rogues, stop pouring that firewater down your collars," von Dodenburg snapped to Matz and Schulze, "you've got work to do."

"Sir?"

"Get a squad and torch this place. I see there are some jerricans of gas over there in the yard."

"Why, sir?" Schulze asked a little surprised. He knew the C.O. was a brave and resourceful soldier, who could be ruthless when the occasion demanded it. But unlike many German commanders he didn't order civilian property to be destroyed for no reason.

"Because we don't want any trace of our having passed this way, Schulze," von Dodenburg answered. "So a fire would look like an accident." He shrugged. "Perhaps the Maquis got drunk as they often do, and set off an accidental fire. That's what I want the *Amis* to think at least when they come down here to check tomorrow morning. And remember," he added after a moment's pause, "we've got to come back this way, I suppose.

I don't want the *Amis* waiting for us when we do. All right, pop to it."

Fifteen minutes later they were on their way, winding their way in second gear into the mountains, while below them the little hamlet burned merrily. Somehow the sight disturbed von Dodenburg as he looked back. He couldn't help thinking that it was as if they had burnt their boats behind them.

Chapter Six

Just before dawn it started to snow. Suddenly the minor country roads were slick and treacherous and the drivers of the four looted trucks had to be very careful as they edged them round the steep bends, straining their eyes in order to see in the poor light cast by the blacked-out headlights. But it wasn't the worsening weather which worried Zander and von Dodenburg; it was their lack of knowledge of just where the Franco-American positions were exactly.

Intelligence had only been able to supply them with the fact that their immediate front was being held by a Japanese-American regiment. But Intelligence hadn't known where the Maquis positions were, nor those of the French Ist Army attached to the Americans.

Twice they had almost blundered into what they took to be French positions, for when they had called out to the men manning the roadblocks they appeared not to understand English. Indeed, von Dodenburg heard one of the sentries, almost obscured by the falling snow, curse grumpily, "*sales cons . . . je veux dormir!*"

At ten when the snowfall had ceased Zander ordered the little convoy off the road and into a forest track. He told the men they could heat up whatever American food they had looted, and while they dropped stiffly to the snow-covered ground, stamping their feet or urinating in steaming yellow gusbes into the bushes, Zander turned to von Dodenburg and said, "Kuno, it's my guess we'll be hitting the main US positions soon. If they are any soldiers at all, they will have dug in on the reverse slope up there." He nodded to the top of the heights.

"I agree. So what's the drill, Heinz?"

"You know how lazy soldiers are, Kuno. In this kind of weather, I am hoping they will stick close to the roads and not venture too deeply into the forest. So," he wiped the dewdrop off the end of his nose with the back of his one hand, "I'd like to find a trail on which we could use the trucks, leading through the forest and over the peak. What do you think, Kuno?"

For a moment von Dodenburg was tempted to ask what their final objective was and what was the point of all this effort. But after a moment's reflection he didn't. Instead he said, "I'll take a small patrol myself, Heinz and see what can be done."

Zander smiled at him. "I thought you'd say that, old house. Thank you. I'd do it myself, but I have my responsibilities." He didn't explain what they were, but von Dodenburg, following the direction of Zander's gaze as he stared at the second truck, knew what those responsibilities were – the mysterious crate and papers in the bulging briefcase.

Von Dodenburg allowed Matz and Schulze to have their meal, though most of it seemed to be in liquid form, then he snapped, "All right you two sauce hounds, let's get on the stick. We're going to do a recce."

Schulze gave a mock moan and whined, "It's allus us old hares who get the shitty end of the stick."

Grimm, standing a few metres away, looked shocked. "How can you talk to a superior officer like that,

Sergeant?" he demanded. "I thought the discipline in the SS was iron-hard?"

"Go and piss in the wind," Schulze answered without rancour.

Grimm flushed angrily. "What did you say? Don't you realize who I am, Sergeant?"

Schulze shrugged carelessly and picked up his machine pistol, as if it were a child's toy. "Yer just a frigging civvie to me, *Kumpel*," he answered easily.

"Why," Grimms eyes bulged and seemed about to pop out of their sockets behind the pince-nez, "I am a director of the Reichsbank and a personal friend of the Führer," he stuttered. "You can't speak like that to me." He turned to von Dodenburg. "*Obersturmbannführer*, are you going to allow that big wretch to speak to me like that. It's disgraceful. The man ought to be court-martialled."

Schulze hawked and spat into the snow, while van Dodenburg smiled lazily. "Court-martialled – out here?" he said. "Listen *Herr Direktor*, that object there," he pointed to an unmoved Schulze, "is what might well come between you and sudden death. So, if I were you, *Herr Direktor*," again he emphasized the title contemptuously, "I'd show some sort of respect for those who have to stand up and fight when the shit starts to fly. All right, you two, follow me."

Minutes later they were plodding up the steep incline, heading for the summit and what lay beyond. Behind them Zander, his own task finished, strode over to a still fuming Grimm. Immediately the latter started to relate angrily how insolent *Scharführer* Schulze had been to him, a "personal friend of the Führer".

Zander stopped him with an upraised hand and a harsh, "Enough of these trivialities, *Herr Direktor*. You don't fully realize what is really at stake, Herr Grimm.

The route taken by The Wotan Mission
Autumn, 1944

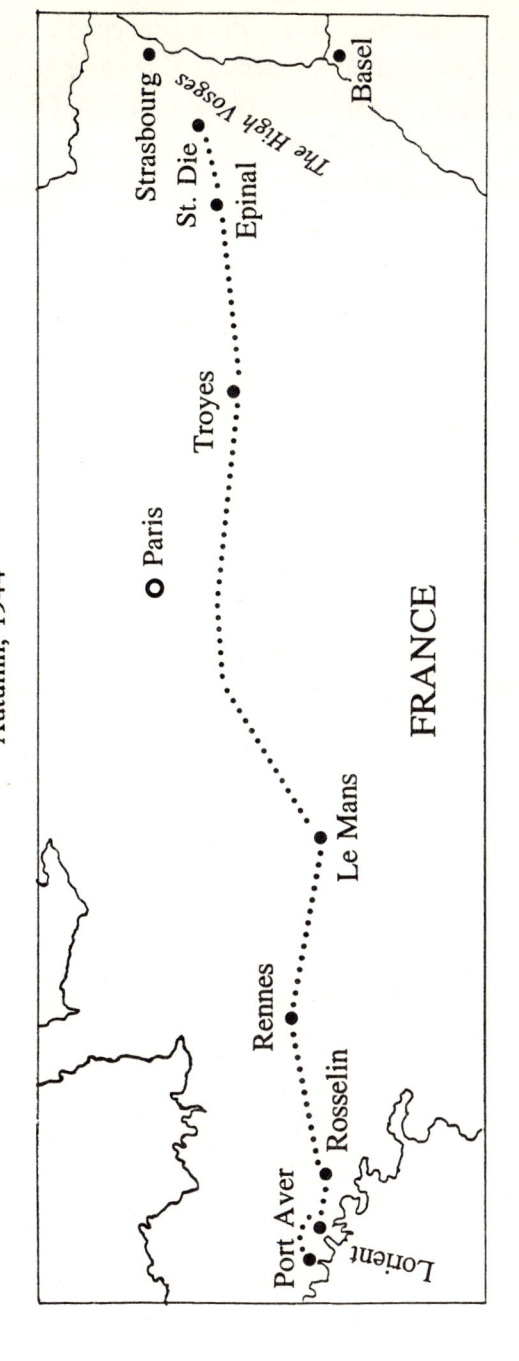

But I'll tell you this. If we don't succeed there can be no future for Germany. Now," he continued, "we are entering the crucial phase of this operation. Once we have passed through the main American line of defence, I think I have a plan which will get us to our destination without too much further difficulty. *But* first we must get through Japs up there. That is vital. Is that understood?"

"Understood," Grimm answered, suddenly subdued, realizing for the first time that he was not in Berlin, where people jumped when he opened his mouth. Here he was very dependent on these rough and ready, surly toughs, who showed him no respect. He bit his bottom lip. Perhaps, he told himself, he should start thinking of his own future, once they reached safety. Perhaps he ought – the thought frightened him too much for him to think it to an end. Yet slowly a new plan was beginning to unfold in his mind. The Third Reich was finished and it meant nothing now that he had once been 'a friend of the Führer'. The time had come to start looking after himself, planning a new life outside a ruined Germany . . .

A kilometre away, von Dodenburg and the two NCOs lay full length in the snow, surveying the Japanese-American positions. As Zander had suspected they occupied both sides of the winding mountain road, securing it with a rough and ready log barricade, covered on both sides by riflemen in foxholes. Further back they had dug in a 57mm anti-tank gun, which was meant to tackle anything attempting to break through the barricade. Then off the road they had erected a wooden shack, from which now smoke curled from a stove pipe. Von Dodenburg, surveying the position through his binoculars, guessed this would be their cookhouse and the place where the off-duty men went to warm up after the freezing air of the mountain peak.

At his side, Schulze whispered, "I make out there are about twenty-five of them including the four men of the anti-tank peashooter of theirs. We could gobble them up for breakfast without even noticing," he added contemptuously. "Frigging lot of little yeller apes."

"I wouldn't be sure," von Dodenburg warned. "Besides, we don't know what the strength they are further down the slope on the other side. No," he lowered his glasses, "the less we have to do with them, the better."

"I don't like that anti-tank gun, sir," Matz ventured. "If those gunners spot us even with that peashooter they could take us out at six hundred metres."

Von Dondeburg frowned. The little one-legged corporal was right. The anti-tank gunners were a real danger to their soft-skinned trucks. Where the trail they had reconnoitred emerged was within easy range of the gun. Any ideas. Matz?" he asked.

"Him and ideas," Schulze said scornfully. "He couldn't even get his rocks off in a whorehouse!"

Matz made an obscene gesture and Schulze said gravely, "Can't, old house, got a double decker bus up there already."

"Hold yer water," von Dodenburg snapped. "What do you think, Matz?"

"We packed a couple of *panzerfausts*." He meant rocket launchers. "I think that just in case, we ought to deal with that anti-tank gun with them. You see, sir, if we came in over there at three o'clock and took the gun out, them yeller apes might think we were just a patrol and while the fur and snot was flying, the trucks could go through at ten o'clock unnoticed." He sniffed and expertly tossed the dewdrop at the end of his red nose into the snow.

Schulze looked at him in mock disdain. "A lot of common people have got into the SS non-commissioned corps these days," he commented.

Von Dodenburg wasn't listening. He liked Matz's bold idea. "But what about you two afterwards?"

Schulze looked aghast. "You mean that little peg-legged horse's ass is volunteering me, sir." He shrugged. "Oh well, somebody's got to look after the little prick. Don't worry. You can't kill weeds that easy. We'll join up with the rest once we've taken the gun out."

Von Dodenburg smiled fondly. How good it was, he thought, to have men like Matz and Schulze serving under him. They certainly weren't parade ground soldiers. In peacetime they would have probably spent most of their time in Torgau Military Prison. But in wartime rogues like these were the salt of the earth. "All right then," he said, "let's get back and sort it out." They started to slither back through the snow to the trail.

Chapter Seven

Slowly, cautiously, the little convoy crawled up the snowbound forest trail towards the summit. Somewhere artillery was firing and the noise of the guns, they hoped, would cover the sound their engines made, labouring upwards in first gear.

Matz and Schulze, hanging onto the running board of the first truck, panzerfaust missile launchers draped over their shoulders, looked at von Dodenburg sitting next to the anxious, pale-faced driver, as he concentrated on getting the truck up to the top. He nodded. As one they dropped off, with Schulze, crying, "If anything goes wrong, sir, make sure I make a pretty corpse."

Von Dodenburg shook his head. "What men?" he said softly to himself. Now as they vanished into the snowbound firs, marching up the mountainside like a regiment of spike-helmeted Prussian grenadiers, he ordered the driver to halt. He had to give Matz and Schulz a chance to get into position before the little convoy breasted the height and was exposed to that dangerous-looking 'peashooter' as Schulze called it.

Now with Schulze helping his one-legged comrade the best he could through the deep snow, their breath coming in grey jets in the freezing air, the two of them emerged from the trees beyond the Japanese-American road barricade. For a moment or two, they crouched there, regaining their breath and watching the little men in their overlarge helmets as they went about their duties, some of them going into the lone hut to emerge bearing canteens of steaming coffee.

"Sadistic sods," Scbulze commented as he watched them drinking the hot coffee. "I could just go a mug of that nigger sweat."

"Stuff it," Matz said cautiously. "Let's get about our business." He flashed a glance at the wrist-watch he had looted from one of the dead Marquis the previous day. "The old man," he meant von Dodenburg, "said, they're going to break out of the forest in ten minutes. Let's haul ass!"

Schulze 'hauled ass' obediently. Keeping their gaze warily on the little yellow men around the barricade, they slid into the forest on the other side of the mountain road and started to work their way to the anti-tank gun.

Now they were some one hundred metres from the anti-tank gun dug in at the side of the road, a pile of shell cases to its rear, with the crew huddled in their greatcoats, stamping their feet and trying to keep warm in the freezing air.

Schulze dropped on to the snow and brought his panzerfaust to bear. "I thought them frigging little yeller apes was on our side," he said. "Well, they was at the beginning back in '41."

"Haven't yer got all yer cups in yer cupboard," Matz commented scornfully. "*Nobody* is on our side." We're losing the frigging war. The days of Greater Germany is over."

"Suppose yer right, old house," Schulze answered a little wearily. "Still yer've got to soldier on, ain't yer."

Matz muttered an impossible anatomical suggestion and lowered himself next to Schulze in the snow, bringing his *panzerfaust* to bear, too. "All right, you first. "If you miss – which yer probably will – I'll take over."

"Show some frigging respect for a senior NCO," Schulze said and peered through the sight of the long hollow tube with the pear-shaped bomb bulging from its muzzle.

Next to him, Matz flung another glance at his watch. "Sixty seconds to go," he announced. "Start the countdown."

Schulze nodded and began to count. "Sixty . . . fifty . . . forty . . ."

Just below the summit von Dodenburg was doing the same, his eyes glued to the second dial of his wrist-watch. Next to him Zander had pulled a stick grenade out of his boot, "just in case," as he had remarked a moment before and was now tensed, ready for what might yet come.

In the third truck, Grimm, his heart beating furiously, told himself he had made the right decision. Once they got out of this mess, he'd carry out his plan. These days people had to look after themselves.

"*Zero!*" von Dodenburg barked. "Roll 'em!"

A grunt, a burst of engine noise and the first truck started to work its way towards the remaining distance to the summit.

From his position Schulze watched as the Japanese-Americans stopped what they were doing, alerted by the sudden noise, and turned in its direction, wondering what was going on. Almost automatically the gunners swung their cannon round in the direction it was coming from. Schulze chuckled and tucking the *panzerfaust* closer to his chin, he cried, "All right, you perverted banana-suckers, *try this one on for size!*" He ripped back the trigger.

The *panzerfaust* erupted flame. For one moment Schulze could see the ugly bomb hissing towards its target, trailing angry fiery-red sparks behind it. There was the hollow clang of metal striking metal. The anti-tank gun sagged to one side as the shield was penetrated and the off-side tyre exploded. Next moment the Japanese-American crew reacted. They bent and started blazing away with their carbines as their attackers advanced.

"What do you want, Matz, a fucking written invite?" Schulze cried, as the slugs started to whack into the snow all about him. "Get them, arse-with-ears!"

Matz needed no urging. He pressed his own trigger. The *panzerfaust* spurted flame. The projectile sped across the snow, blackening it with its heat as it hurtled towards its target. Again there was that hollow boom of metal slamming into metal. The anti-tank groaned and rolled to its side.

Next instant the shell in the gun's breech exploded. The barrel split like a rotten banana and the crew flew into the air, their blood splattering the snow all around in great scarlet gobs. Schulze dropped his one-shot weapon and picked up his machine pistol. "All right, you little cripple, hobble off toot sweet. I'll give you covering fire for a minute." He pressed the Schmeisser's trigger and swinging his big body from left to right, he hosed the area to his immediate front.

But Schulze had not reckoned with the reckless bravery of these little Japanese-Americans. Despite the heavy fire, they ran across the snow, waving their weapons, crying, "*Banzai.*" Men went down on sides, cut down by that merciless fire. But that didn't seem to stop them. Even the wounded attempted to get up again and hobble after their cheering comrades.

Schulze's magazine clicked. It was empty. "Bugger this

for a game of soldiers," he cursed. With his free hand he pulled out one of looted egg-shaped American grenades. He tugged out the pin with his teeth. Then he threw it at the attacking Japanese-Americans with all his might. Next moment he was stumbling furiously through the snow into the trees after Matz, as the first of the trucks emerged from the forest to the stalled Nisei's rear . . .

That evening they halted in a ruined abandoned French village on the other side of the mountains. Everywhere shellfire had destroyed the medieval houses' roofs and the walls were pockmarked with shrapnel like the symptoms of some loathsome skin disease.

Still the ruined houses offered some protection from the biting cold and von Dodenburg told himself, as he personally posted the first sentries that there'd probably be snow before the night was over.

It was nearly three hours since they had last heard gunfire and as Zander said, "It looks as if we've outrun the Nips. I suspect we're virtually through the *Amis'* main line of resistance. Of course there'll be supply units to come and the like, but nothing that should prove a serious challenge to us."

Schulze who had overheard the crippled SS General's remark had observed thereupon to Matz, "The only challenge that Mrs Schulze's son wants at this moment is some suds and something to scoff. My stomach's doing back flips with hunger. Come on, apeturd, let's see what we can scrounge."

While the two old hares set about finding something to scrounge, von Dodenburg walked into the *mairie*, as battered as the other houses, but with its roof intact, which Zander was using as his personal HQ. Grimm was nowhere in sight, but von Dodenburg suspected he was out looking after his truck and its mysterious contents.

Zander looked tired as he slumped in the vanished mayor's moth-eaten armchair, his boots off, trying to warm his frozen feet at the miserable little fire which someone had lit for him in the grate. Formally von Dodenburg saluted and Zander forced a weary grin, saying, "For Chrissake, Kuno, don't be so frigging regimental. We're not back in Berlin now, you know." He indicated the other chair. "Take the weight off your feet, old house."

Gratefully von Dodenburg sat down on the only other chair in the shabby wrecked office. Outside all was silent now, save for the steady tread of the sentry outside on the crisp frozen snow. Zander nodded to the pack of looted American cigarettes on the table. "Help yourself to a lung torpedo, Kuno," he said, "I've got something to say to you."

Von Dodenburg did as he was commanded and waited, watching Zander's face in the flickering reflection of the fire which hollowed it out to a hard death's head. "Where's the fire?" he asked after a while, when Zander still didn't speak.

"Oh just a few thoughts. The *Amis* will have tumbled to the fact by now that we are behind their lines and I'm sure they have the intelligence to ask themselves what we're doing here. I am certain it won't be long before they started sending out patrols to look for us. Perhaps as early as dawn tomorrow. So we'll have to get rid of the trucks. They are a dead giveaway."

Von Dodenburg nodded his understanding and puffed at his cigarette, the blue smoke wreathing his lean face.

"But we'll need the trucks until we get out of the High Vosges," Zander continued. "Then we must find some other form of transport because we still have a long journey in front of us." He frowned as if he had just remembered how long it was.

"Just what is our destination?" Von Dodenburg ventured.

Zander didn't reply. Instead he asked a question of his own. "Straight from the shoulder now, Kuno? Do you really think we can win the war any longer?"

Von Dodenburg hesitated. He stared into the weak, flickering flame in the grate, as if he might find the answer there. Zander waited patiently. Outside, some way off someone had begun laughing loudly. Von Dodenburg sucked his teeth thoughtfully and said, "No, I don't think we can still win. But I *do* think we can make it so hard for the Allies to achieve victory that they'll give us better terms than that unconditional surrender which Roosevelt has offered the German people."

Zander nodded. "I agree with you on both counts, Kuno. But what if I told you we have the means to produce a terrible new weapon," he held up his one arm in warning, "don't ask me any more about it ... but with this weapon, if it can be made we will get those terms we want."

Von Dodenburg whistled softly, impressed. "But," he asked a moment later, face puzzled. "But what have we to do with this new weapon, Heinz?"

We are taking the plans of it and other material to those who will – hopefully – finally make that terrible weapon," Zander answered carefully. "There is a Jap submarine waiting to take them on board on the French coast."

"The French coast!"

"Yes."

"Where?"

"I'm afraid I can't tell you that. But we must do it. Perhaps Germany's future depends upon it. If the Western Allies threaten to turn Germany into one great farm, with our menfolk little better than agricultural labourers, then we must destroy the Western Allies *totally*!"*

He stopped speaking and the two of them simply sat there in the growing darkness, each man wrapped in a cocoon of his own thoughts – and they weren't pleasant . . .

---

* The US Morgenthau Plan envisaged destroying Germany's industrial base after an Allied victory. *Transl.*

Part Two

THE V-MAIL EXPRESS

Chapter One

Captain Hurd, Royal Marines, pulled down his balaclava, touched his face to check whether the camouflage cream was still there and whispered, "All right, Corporal, shove the folboat over the side." He turned to the captain of the little fishing smack which had brought them to the mouth of the estuary and added softly, "*Merci, mon capitaine.*"

"*Bonne chance*," the skipper, who stank of garlic and stale fish, whispered back. He combined fishing off the stretch of enemy-held coastline with a little discreet spying for the local maquis. Now he would wait with his nets out for fifteen minutes before starting his engines and alerting the German coastal watchers at Lorient that there was someone just off the port. By then Captain Hurd hoped to be in position off the submarine pens.

Now Hurd and Corporal 'Chalky' White slid themselves into the folding boat and, on command from the SBS commander, started to wield their paddles, both their gazes fixed on the stark black outline of the besiege port. No light showed in the port for it was well after curfew and the Germans enforced a strict blackout. But occasionally a white beam stabbed the freezing darkness as the German searchlight crews searched the estuary for mines, frogmen and saboteurs.

It had been over a month now since the Americans

had launched a company-sized attack on the place, but despite the quietness of this remote front, the German defenders were very much on their toes. Indeed, Hurd told himself, as he paddled powerfully but silently towards their objective, the Germans had increased their vigilance of late. It seemed to show that something was afoot.

Once the searchlight swept in their direction. "*Duck*," Hurd hissed urgently.

The Corporal reacted immediately. They were both old hands. They had been on ops with the Special Boat Service since its formation back in '41. They knew exactly what to do. Both stopped paddling and lay with their upper bodies pressed against the canvas of the folboat. The light swept over them and then went on. Still they didn't move. It was an old trick. A moment later the icy white light swept back to them. But then the searchlight operators seemed satisfied that it was only a log they had spotted. Suddenly the light went out altogether, leaving them blinded for a few moments in the sudden darkness.

Ten minutes later, as out in the bay the French skipper started up the engine of his ancient fishing boat, the two of them were nosing their frail craft against the jetty, using their hands now to do so instead of the paddles; the latter made too much noise. Somewhere above there was the clatter of drums and then the sound of a squeaky accordion playing *bal musette* music, interspersed with raucous female laughter. "Somebody having a bit of a do with the local tarts, boss," Chalky White ventured, "lucky for some."

"You get your share, you evil man," Hurd whispered back with a grin. He stopped short. In the faint light he caught the glint of metal, and a tiny red glimmer.

A sentry was standing in a doorway some twenty yards away having what White would have called, 'a crafty spit-and-a-draw'.

"Nobble him," he ordered tensely, as they made the boat stop.

"Righto, sir," the corporal replied, as if it was every day that he murdered sentries in cold blood.

While Hurt held the boat, White clambered up the jetty wall noiselessly and effortlessly like a monkey. Minutes later there was a soft stifled moan, followed by a muted clatter and the sentry disappeared from view. One more minute and there was a splash as White dropped the body into the harbour. "Coast clear," he called down in a hoarse whisper, not even breathing hard.

Hurriedly Hurd tied up the boat. He, too, swung himself up the jetty wall effortlessly.

"Poor sod," White commented as they crouched there in the freezing darkness. "Didn't know what hit him. Didn't look a day over sixteen."

Hurd shrugged. Human life didn't mean much to him any more. Besides, he knew if the Germans caught him and White, they would stand them up against the nearest wall and shoot them out of hand. Hitler had ordered his men to do that to all captured SAS and SBS men. "Come on, let's have a scout round, Chalky," he ordered. "Can't stand here like a spare dildo in a convent."

"Right sir."

Noiselessly in their rubber-soled shoes, sticking close to the shadow cast by the battered, shell pocked buildings, the two of them started to work their way in the direction from which the noise was coming.

"Here we are, sir," the Corporal said. "Their blackout ain't too hot. There's a chink in the curtain here—" he stopped short as he peered into the room from which the noise was coming. "Cor ferk a duck, sir!" he breathed in awe. "They ain't half up to some high jinks in there. Have a butcher's, sir." He moved to one side so that Hurd could look in.

He whistled softly at what he could see. A naked girl was dancing drunkenly on a table, clad only in sheer black stockings. But it wasn't her nakedness that caught him by surprise; it was the fact that her pubic thatch had been coloured red and white, the colour of the flag of Japan, the rising sun.

Now a group of very drunken Japanese officer were shaking bottles of champagne and directing the jets of fizzy wine at her pubes, laughing crazily as they did so. Behind them there were drunken Japanese everywhere, some of they lying in their own vomit, others already copulating with the French whores on tables, chairs, even on the floor. On the coatrack by the door an unconscious Japanese officer hung by his braces, head lolled to one side, snoring heavily.

"By Christ, you're right, Chalky," Hurd breathed. "They're having a life of Reilly all right. Well, one thing, we now know these must be the Nips who brought that sub in the other day."

"Yessir. But that doesn't tell us much more. They'll need to know more than that back in London. You know what their Lordships are, when they want information. They want it PDQ."

"Yes, pretty damned quick is the phrase." Hurd was thoughtful for a moment, as the racket continued inside. The naked girl had fallen into the lap of one of the Japanese officers and already he was fumbling drunkenly to open his flies. "Listen, Chalky, are you game for a risk?" Hurd asked.

"I wouldn't be here if I wasn't, sir," the other man whispered back.

"All right, let's try to nobble one of those drunken Nips and take him back with us to base. They're all pretty small. We could get him into the folboot."

"First yer've got to catch the bugger. We can't just walk in there and nab one of them, sir."

"We're not going to, Chalky. We're going to let him come to us."

"How do you mean, sir?"

"Well, the Nips pass water the same way as we do – and by the way they're knocking back the wallop I think they'll need to urinate at pretty frequent intervals."

"Got yer, sir," Chalky White said urgently. "So what we need to do is the find that knocking shop's *pissoir*."

"Exactly." Hurd allowed himself a taut smile. "I can see you haven't been wasting your time out here in France. *Pissoir* indeed! Come on, let's go."

They found the primitive lavatory easily. The stink was all too obvious. Hastily they concealed themselves in the shadows and waited, with Chalky White holding his lead cosh at the ready. Almost immediately they heard footsteps approaching the place. But then they heard drunken voices and realized that there were at least two of the Japanese – too many for them to tackle.

The Japanese swayed drunkenly back to the French brothel and again they waited in the freezing cold, their hearts beating rapidly with the pent-up tension.

The minutes passed leadenly. In the upper storey of the old house bed springs were creaking rustily. "Someone's going at it like a frigging fiddler's elbow—" White began. Suddenly his tone changed to one of urgent expectancy. "Someone's coming, sir. There's something clanking like."

Hurd chanced a look. A stocky little figure was swaying dangerously from side to side as he came toward the latrine, trailing an enormous sabre behind on the cobbles of the courtyard – and he was alone.

"Christ, what does he want a toothpick like that for in a knocking shop?" White hissed.

"Don't know. We'll ask him once we've nobbled him."

"Shall we let him have his Jimmy Riddle first?" White asked in high good humour.

"Better. He won't have much chance to pee in the folboot. Get ready. Here comes the little sod now."

They clung to the shadows, hardly daring to breathe as the little officer staggered by them, fiddling already with his flies. Despite the cold, White could feel the hand holding the cosh was abruptly wet with sweat. He licked his lips.

Inside the latrine there came the sound of hot gushing urine followed by the sound of the little man breaking wind loudly and exclaiming, "ah", as if it had given him pleasure. There was the clanking sound again as he turned and started to come out. He didn't get far. White sprang from the shadows, cosh raised. He slammed it down on the Japanese's bare shaven head. He gave a quiet grunt and his knees started to buckle beneath him like those of a newly born foal. Hurd caught him just before he smashed to the ground and lowered him gently to the freezing cobbles.

"Get that sabre off him," he ordered.

"Thought we might keep it as a souvenir," White objected.

"No room for it in the folboot."

Swiftly White undid the great sword. Then, with a grunt, Hurd heaved the unconscious officer over his shoulder, pistol, with silencer attached, in his right hand. "Come on, Chalky. Let's get cracking, before they miss the little Nip."

White needed no urging.

Sticking to the shadows they crept down the silent blacked-out streets, every sense highly acute, eyes peering through the darkness for the first sign of danger. But they encountered none. They could have been the last people alive in the world. They reached the jetty where they had tied their little craft. White went down first. Hastily Hurd lowered his unconscious burden to him. "It's gonna be a bit tight," White whispered as he stowed their prisoner in the folboat. "And this Nip doesn't half smell a bit ripe."

"Get on with it," Hurd hissed, eyes searching the darkness, pistol at the ready.

Suddenly, startlingly, the prisoner moaned out loud. A few feet a harsh voice cried, "*Halt . . . wer da?*"

"Christ, that's torn it White snapped.

Hurd acted instinctively. As a dark shape, carrying a bayonetted rifle came into view, he fired, praying that his bullet wouldn't go too high.

It didn't. There was a soft noise. A scream and then the Sentry went tumbling to the cobbles, his rifle making a hell of a noise as it clattered down.

Hurd jumped. He slammed into the boat and made it rock wildly. Next to him, White clubbed his fist and smashed it into the Japanese's face. He went out like a light once more. Then with the sirens sounding their urgent warnings, harsh voices shouting orders and searchlights clicking on everywhere along the estuary, the two Marines were paddling for their lives.

Chapter Two

Commander Fleming and the woman interpreter arrived in France at dawn. Immediately they were driven from the airport down the slick, gleaming white roads to the SBS's little base on the coast where they were holding their prisoner.

Fleming had had little sleep the previous night, ever since he had heard the news that Hurd had carried out a daring mission into Lorient and had actually managed to take a Japanese officer prisoner. There had been a flight to organize and a Japanese interpreter to be found.

Now she snoozed quietly beside him in the back seat of the big American Packard, slight and bespectacled and prettyish in an oriental way, though when her eyes were open they gave the impression of great intelligence and daring – there was no other word Fleming could find to describe the look.

She was a senior lecturer at the London School of Oriental Languages and he had been told over the phone by her professor that it had taken great determination on her part to become what she was. "Japanese women are supposed to stay at home, Fleming, and serve their lord and master, their husband. They are not expected to study and take up a profession."

When she had been asked whether she was prepared to fly to France to help in the interrogation of an important

Japanese prisoner, she had replied immediately without any fuss, "Have me picked up within the hour. I shall be ready for you, commander." Nor had she asked any questions about their mission, saying simply, "I shall be your mouthpiece, Commander Fleming, that is all." Then she had gone effortlessly to sleep in the noisy Dakota taking them to France.

Now it was quite light and, as the Packard came ever closer to the sea, Fleming could see there had been heavy fighting in the area a while back. There were rusting tanks and abandoned guns on both sides of the road and the fields were still marked with great shell holes where the local farmers had still not filled them in.

Fleming dismissed the scenery and ran his mind over what he had got already. It wasn't much. But the chief point was, he told himself, that the Japanese had sent a valuable large cargo-carrying sub to Lorient, which was obviously going to be used to transport something away from the besieged *port*. That something had to be important, very important, for the Japs to risk the sub. This day he was going to find out by hook or by crook what that cargo was.

Fifteen minutes later Captain Hurd was explaining what had happened the night before, while they both drank tea laced with Issue rum to take the chill out of their bones. Mrs Smith (for she had been married to an Englishman who had been killed in Burma two years before; he, too, had been a Japanese specialist) listened intently, her face solemn and passive, but when Hurd was finished, she said quietly in her excellent English, "He is going to be a tough nut to crack. He has lost face already and he must be guarded well at all times. For he will attempt to kill himself out of shame."

Hurd smiled softly as he stood with his back to red-hot

stove. "At this time he is still nursing a very severe headache, I can assure you, but he *is* being guarded by one of my corporals. A very good man, who won't stand any nonsense."

She nodded her understanding. "Tie his one hand up to something, leaving the other free. Feed him some food and see what his reaction is," she suggested.

Fleming looked at the little Oriental woman in slight bewilderment. "Why? The best way to break a prisoner down quickly is to deprive him of food, drink and sleep, Mrs Smith."

"Because if he eats something, it will show he is still undecided about taking his life and is still co-operating. That's what we want, isn't it?'

Fleming beamed at her. "What smart thinking, Mrs Smith. We'll have that done straight away."

Ten minutes later Corporal White came in, saluted and reported with more formality than he used ordinarily with Captain Hurd, "Beg to report, sir, that the Oriental gentleman has eaten a banger, a slice of fried bread, bit of scrambled egg and has supped a mug of Sarnt-Major's char."

Hurd winked at him and said, "All right then, bring him in and we'll begin."

Outside it was beginning to snow again, the snow coming straight in from the sea, bitter and cold, so that when White opened the door to usher in the prisoner, Mrs Smith shuddered involuntarily in the sudden cold.

He was a small man, about twenty-five, and he looked decidedly under the weather, but his face was tough and his eyes revealed nothing but sullen caution. Because of Mrs Smith's warning, the young Japanese lieutenant's hands were tied behind his back with another rope leading from the bound hands to a noose around his neck.

The officer looked around at his captors. Then he saw the woman and for a moment his slant-eyed face showed some animation. He must have guessed that she was the interpreter for he said, "Me no speak English." This he followed with a staccato burst of Japanese directed at the woman.

She bowed, gave him a fake smile and said out of the side of her mouth to Fleming, "He's just said to me, 'Don't you dare talk to me, you daughter of a whore. Content yourself with letting the foreign devils stick it into you.'"

Fleming's face hardened. "That young man needs to be taught a lesson in politeness," he said grimly.

"He will be," she answered, still bowing and giving the prisoner that fake smile of a stupid obedient woman. "He will, Commander."

She stopped bowing, but kept her eyes averted humbly, as if she were a person of no importance in front of this Japanese naval officer.

As Captain Hurd watched curiously, Fleming took out one of his Bond Street cigarettes deliberately and inserted it in his long ivory cigarette holder and lit it. Then he said, "Ask why he came to Lorient."

Mrs Smith said something in Japanese, still keeping her gaze low.

The little Japanese officer looked annoyed, but said nothing.

"Tell him we know all about his I-Class submarine and that it can carry cargo. Was it bringing cargo in or was it to take cargo out of Lorient?"

Mrs Smith translated Fleming's question, while the Japanese officer looked at her, his face impassive. But when she had finished, his face darkened angrily and he stamped his right foot. He let go with a burst of angry Japanese.

"What did he say?" Fleming enquired eagerly.

"He said, he was a Japanese officer of the Imperial Japanese Navy and he would rather be dead than betray his Majesty, the Emperor's secrets."

"He's going to be a tough nut," Hurd commented. "But we can't beat it out of him like the Japs do to our people."

For the first time since the Japanese prisoner had been brought it, Mrs Smith raised her gaze. She looked from Fleming to the SBS officer and said very quietly, "I think even if you did beat him you'd get nothing out of him. By his speech I take him to be one of those tough peasant boys who had the luck to be sent to naval college and become an officer. He talks about *bushido* the Japanese code of honour, but he's no gentleman. But remember, Commander Fleming, he was tough to start with, and all the years he was a rating and then a midshipman until he became an officer, he was beaten by his superiors all the time for the slightest offence. So he is used to being knocked about." She hesitated for a moment, then said, "But there is one possible way of getting him – to, er spill the bean." She smiled slightly at her use of the phrase.

Fleming took his ivory holder out of his somewhat thin, cruel-looking lips. "How?" he demanded.

"Humiliate him by making him take off his clothes. Japanese men are accustomed to very lax behaviour but they don't particularly like being looked at naked by strangers, especially white people." She coughed delicately and smiled again. "They are particularly sensitive about the size of their organs. They think white men have much larger ones, you see."

Hurd guffawed and Fleming exclaimed, "Well, I'll be

damned! You're a real card, Mrs Smith. I think we could use you in Intelligence. Well, let's give it a go. Corporal, take the clothes off that officer please."

White hesitated a moment then he grabbed for the Japanese officer's tunic. The latter looked at him puzzled. But White didn't give him a chance to be awkward. He grabbed the tunic at the collar and ripped it off the little yellow man. The shirt followed, while the Japanese squirmed and wriggled, but White was too strong for him. Off came the shirt and singlet. A moment later White had whipped off the Japanese officer's long drawers and he stood there naked, face burning with shame, hands held in front of his private parts.

"Just like a virgin, caught with her knickers down," a triumphant White exclaimed and then realizing that Mrs Smith was present, he added hastily, "Very sorry I said that, Mrs Smith." Now it was his turn to go red.

"All's fair in love and war," she commented easily. "Now them, Commander, I shall ask him your question once again, promising him his clothes back if he tells us – and it's true. But after this you'd better watch him like a hawk. After this humiliation, he'll commit suicide at the first opportunity." She turned to the shamefaced Japanese officer, his skinny frame trembling with suppressed rage and indignation. Rapidly she posed Fleming's question in Japanese once more, adding that he would be given back his uniform if he answered truthfully.

The prisoner pressed his lips firmly together, as if willing himself not to speak. He shook his head vehemently.

Mrs Smith remained calm and in control of the situation. She said, "Gentlemen, would you look directly at his loins. Corporal pull away his hands."

White answered, "Yes ma'am", and with a swift gesture

pulled the prisoner's hands behind his back. The Japanese was caught by surprise. He gasped something and then flushed even more as both Fleming and Hurd looked pointedly at his naked loins.

"Now," Mrs Smith said in Japanese, "tell me what I need to know. Then you get your clothes."

The Japanese officer's eyes brimmed over with tears of rage and shame. His whole body trembled violently, as if he were having a fit. Words came from his mouth in tight little groups, always followed by what might be a gasp of regret.

Mrs Swift's face lit up as she translated. "He's saying that they brought some items from Japan for Germany's war industry ... tungsten, ball bearings, industrial diamonds and the like. The stuff they used to get from Sweden and can't get now ..."

Fleming looked disappointed. "Is that all?"

"No, there was something more important."

"What?" Fleming demanded, eyes gleaming now as he bit at his ivory holder as if he might well bite right through it.

"They are to sail immediately once an important cargo gets through the American siege. First they are to sail with some of that cargo to South America."

Fleming whistled softly. "So the rats are deserting the sinking ship. They're getting their fortunes out to South America. But what are the Nips – er – Japanese getting out of it?"

Mrs Smith repeated his question, while White held on to the prisoner firmly.

He bowed his head in shame and whispered so that she had to strain to hear him. "Something which might change the war," she translated. "That's all he knows. Something that—"

Suddenly the Japanese lashed with his foot at White's groin. The Corporal was caught completely by surprise. He let go. The naked prisoner didn't hesitate. He dived at the door, wrenched it open and then he was running all out for the cliff and the sea beyond. "Stop that man!" Hurd bellowed urgently.

Marines stopped their work. A couple raised their rifles and Fleming cried, "Don't shoot. Tackle him somebody!"

A lanky marine started to race after the fleeing prisoner. He began to gain on him, but the cliff edge was looming up ever closer. Fleming was desperate. He knew what the Jap was going to do. He was going to fling himself off it, to the shingle beach far below. He was going to kill himself. "Run," he cried. "Run, man, *run!*"

Too late. With one last gasped "*Banzai*", both arms raised in a final salute to the Emperor, the little prisoner flung himself over and disappeared from sight. His heart stopped with overwhelming fear. He was dead before he smashed into the wet shingle. "Brave little bastard," was Hurd's only comment when they turned him over and looked at his smashed dead face. "Brave little bastard . . ."

Chapter Three

Now they were emerging from the High Vosges. The going was still slick and treacherous and the drivers drove their vehicles in second gear. But the snow on the ground was not so deep as in the mountains and here and there there were patches completely free.

Schulze and Matz were up front in the first truck with von Dodenburg, Matz at the wheel, with the two others holding their machine pistols at the ready. For about two kilometres ahead, outlined against the leaden, snow-heavy sky, they could see the onion-tower of a baroque church, surrounded by a straggle of medieval houses, whose tall chimneys bore the great empty stork nets typical of Alsace. Here and there blue smoke streamed from a chimney. Otherwise they couldn't make out any sign of life. Perhaps the place had been evacuated during the fighting, von Dodenburg reasoned.

At his side, Schulze, quite unmoved by the fact that they might be heading for trouble, was saying to Matz, "Yer know I was once a virgin. In fact I was a virgin for a long time, right till I was eight or nine."

He frowned at himself in the driving mirror, as if he couldn't comprehend why it had taken 'Mrs Schulze's handsome son' all that time till he succumbed to the pleasures of the flesh. "I mean I had plenty of opportunities. Our neighbour was Fraulein Dockweiler. She was a pavement pounder. She worked the Jungfernstieg just off the Alster in Hamburg. She was allus inviting me into her flat when she was undressed, flashing her milk factory at me and telling me what a handsome lad I was. In fact, my old dad used to say, when he was sober that was, "laddie, I fancy a slice of that gash mesen, but she fancies you," and he'd scratch his poor head and dance the old mattress polka with my mother. Queer ain't it. A virgin till I was eight. Nowadays I've just got to look at a piece of gash and I get a diamond cutter straight off. That reminds me—"

"I ain't had it so long I've got so much ink in me fountain pen, I don't know who to write to first," Matz beat him to it.

Von Dodenburg barked, "Knock it off. I think there's *Amis* in that village. Look."

He pointed to their front. A truck, an American truck, was moving slowly out of the village, towing a trailer behind it, heading west towards the plains beyond.

Schulze pulled out the American forty-five they had been given, together with the US uniforms and laid it in his lap. "If there's trouble, somebody's gonna get a sudden headache," he said grimly.

"Yes, but we don't want trouble if we can avoid it. Today we want to ditch these trucks, according to *Standartenfuhrer* Zander and find some other means of transport. We don't want to draw any attention to ourselves. All right, wooden eye be on your guard."

Now they could see several soldiers moving around the village, and wires had been strung along skeletal trees leading from the place on the side of the road, indicating, von Dodemburg told himself, that the place was linked with another enemy unit. If anything was to happen, it had to happen fast and furious so that the Americans had no opportunity to radio for help.

They rolled ever closer. They came level with the first houses. A black soldier looked out at the trucks from an open doorway. He saw the white soldiers and suddenly looked worried.

"Don't the US Army have any white stubble hoppers?" Matz asked. "First yellow Japs and now black?"

"Shut up," von Dodenburg snapped. "Did you see the look on the feller's face. He's worried about something."

"If I polished his visage for him, he *would* be worried," Schulze said dourly.

They rolled on, nerves jingling electrically.

The market squre was about a hundred metres ahead. A long line of black soldiers stood in the snow, waiting outside a house, the men laughing and joking, each of them carrying cans and cartons of cigarettes in their hands. A black MP in a white-painted helmet, swinging a white club, walked up and down, supervising them.

"What in three devils' name is going on?" von Dodenburg asked.

Schulze licked his lips, as if he were preparing to eat a big meal. "I wonder if it could be a knocking shop? I could—"

"Shut up!" von Dodenburg broke in harshly. "I think we've been rumbled."

To their right a black officer, wearing a steel helmet and with a pistol in a leather holster on his belt, was eyeing them. His face was serious, and von Dodenburg couldn't help thinking he looked suspicious.

"Shall I drop him?" Schulze rasped, the prospect of the knocking shop forgotten.

"Not yet. Let's see," von Dodenburg answered. He

prayed that the troopers in the following trucks were already alert to the danger they were in. Now the serious-looking black officer was walking down the steps, his hand on his pistol holster, as if he were going to inspect the trucks more carefully.

Schulze cocked the hammer of the pistol on his lap. He felt instinctively that something was going to happen soon.

The serious-looking officer shouted something to the line of black men waiting outside in the house in the snow. The MP, watching them turned smartly. He saluted and then started to march into the centre of the street, club raised.

"Great crap on the Christmas tree!" Matz cursed. "He wants us to stop. What am I to do, sir?"

"Stop," von Dodenburg answered, "honk your horn to alert the others." He pulled out and cocked his own '45, and added grimly, "Prepare for trouble."

Matz flashed a smile at the big, self-important MP and changed down gear. "All right, snowdrop," he said grimly, "you've asked for this."

To their right, the serious-looking officer was looking more relaxed now. Things seemed to be going all right. He was thinking that obviously.

Matz braked. The MP took his time, showing off in front of the line of black soldiers. Here he was, a black military policeman stopping a white convoy, being led, so it appeared, by an officer wearing twin silver bars of a captain. He tapped his club on the bonnet officiously to indicate that the master sergeant, who was Schulze, should wind down his side window, not knowing that by doing so he had signed his own death warrant. Behind the lead trucks, the others started to slow down.

Schulze wound the window down.

The big black shining face looked at him, "'Kay, Sarge, let's see some I.D," the MP said.

Schulze didn't understand a word. What he did understand was that the time had come for action. He lifted the pistol. The man contorted with terror. "Hey," he cried, "what—" Schule fired. The MP's face disintegrated like a soft-boiled egg being struck by a too heavy spoon. The black turned a gory scarlet, through which the teeth gleamed like polished ivory. He reeled back, dead before he hit the snow-covered cobbles.

Next instant all hell broke loose. The line of Negroes were caught completely by surprise. They went down like ninepins. The black officer fell to one knee and pulled out his Colt. He started zipping off well-aimed shots to left and right. Not for long. A burst of automatic fire ripped the front of his chest to bloody pieces. He flung up his arms, as if appealing to God to show him some mercy. But God was looking the other way on this cold, cruel morning. Another burst hit him in the stomach and bowled him over so that he lay outstretched in the snow, as if he had been crucified.

Now the SS troopers were springing from their trucks, firing as they jumped. Negroes went down everywhere. Already, even though some of their comrades were sniping the attackers from the upper windows of the houses on both sides of the street, many were surrendering, taking off their helmets for some strange reason known only to themselves and crying in terror, the only word of German they knew, "*Kamerad* . . . don't shoot *Kamerad*!"

Von Dodenburg opened his mouth to order the ceasefire when his ears were assailed by the rumble of tank tracks. The next instant a white painted Sherman tank rattled around the corner, its tracks flinging up the snow, its long hooded gun already swinging round to bear on the stalled trucks. "Well, I'll piss in my boot!" Schulze cried, stopping firing with surprise.

"*Ram it!*" von Dodenburg yelled above the snap and crackle of the fire fight.

"What, sir?" Matz began in the same instant that muzzle of cannon belched flame. The shell exploded only metres away. Shrapnel flew everywhere, ripping the truck's canvas as it rocked back and forth wildly with the blast.

"*Ram the bastard!*" von Dodenburg shrieked.

Matz flung home first gear and let go of the clutch. The truck raced forward, scattering black soldiers to left and right, its tyres bouncing over the dead and dying lying in the street.

The Sherman fired again. The windscreen burst into a gleaming spider's web. Grimly Matz kept going, sweat suddenly streaming down his ashen face, as he gripped the wheel in white-knuckled fear.

Another shell struck the street in front of them. Schulze yelped as a piece of red-hot shrapnel slammed into his arm. "Bugger this for a tale!" he cried and fired a burst at the Sherman's tough metal hide. Bullets whined off the armour harmlessly. But they obviously rattled the gunner for his next shell was well wide of the mark.

Now with fascinated horror, Matz crouched over the wheel, saw the Sherman fill the whole horizon, as he raced forward on his lethal collision course. He spotted the pale face of the driver in his hatch, knowing that he, too, was powerless to do anything. Fate had taken over.

Crump . . . crash! With a great rending tearing snarl, the two vehicles, the thirty-ton tank and the two-and-a-half-ton truck slammed into each other. The truck's whole bonnet crumpled. The air was full of the cloying stench of petrol as its petrol tank exploded.

"*Out!*" Matz heard von Dodenburg cry urgently through the red mist that threatened to overcome him. Weakly he opened the buckled door and fell into the snow. Behind him in the truck the men were doing the same.

Schulze grabbed hold of him by the collar. "Come on, apeturd, move yer ass . . . she's going up."

Next instant the truck's engine burst into flame. A great blowtorch of flame seared the length of the tank and the men trapped inside it began to scream. The cries seemed to go on for ever, as the Sherman's paint started to bubble and plop with that tremendous heat. And then at last it was over and there was nothing but a loud echoing silence that rang and rang in the circle of hills, as if there would never be an end to it.

Chapter Four

Schulze and Matz looked at the women who had been servicing the black soldiers. They looked hard and tough, their raddled faces painted a flaming red, their lips scarlet slashes. In their turn, they stared back at the two German soldiers with professional eagerness, opening their mouths, licking their lips slowly and suggestively, feeling inside their low-cut dresses and fondling a breast, as if they couldn't get to the business of sex soon enough.

"They've had black dicks inside o' them," Matz warned.

Schulze shrugged. "It don't worry me if they had green and purple dicks inside of 'em. They're beaver ain't they? And I'd like part o' some o' that beaver before we're on our way to God knows where agen."

"No money, no beaver," a hard voice boomed behind them.

The two of them swung round surprised. A big woman had come down the stairs behind them, dyed jet-black hair piled high on her head, huge breasts trembling like jelly beneath the thin material of her black silk blouse. She spread her outstretched hands in a kind of a circle in front of her lower abdomen. "You understand me, boys?"

Schulze licked suddenly dry lips. He told himself it would be worth a few Hail Marys to commit a sin with her. Next to him, Matz said out of the side of his mouth, "Just my collar size that one."

The big woman looked at him coldly with calculating eyes. "No tickee, no washee," she said. "Get it?"

The German was accented, but it was the kind of racy German the average soldier would use and Schulze asked, "Are you German?"

The woman threw back her head and laughed, her breasts trembling mightily as she did so. "German ... French ... American ... I'm everything, soldier boy. I'm *Mariposa ... Papillon ... Schmetterling* ... Butterfly for anyone who can pay me and my girls." She indicated the whores, who now looked fearful, as if they were a little scared of the big woman.

"Butterfly?" Schulze asked puzzled.

She grinned at him, showing him a mouthful of gleaming white teeth, with here and there the gleam of gold. "Butterfly because when men do it with me – their knees tremble," she explained.

"Mine are trembling already," Schulxe admitted. "But why standing up – er – Butterfly?"

She looked at him proudly, throwing out that magnificent chest of hers. "Why? Because I won't go down under a man – for anything. *Klar*?"

"*Klar*," Schulze answered hurriedly.

The woman looked at the two of them shrewdly and asked, "What are you German boys doing here behind the *Ami* lines? I thought you'd left France for good. I mean when you were here, you were all right. Business was good. But the *Amis* pay better. Funny lot, though. They don't want fuckee-fuckee." she made an explicit gesture with her fingers. "They all seem to want suckee-suckee. Perhaps they don't get any of that in their country." She shrugged carelessly and those breasts of hers trembled wildly beneath the sheer black silk.

Schulze licked his lips at the sight, like a man who was longing wildly for a drink and said, "Just a mission."

"What kind of a mission?" she asked.

"Can't tell you, Butterfly," Matz said importantly. "Top secret. Only us senior NCOs know what it is."

"Put a sock in it," Schulze snapped sharply. "Don't let's waste time. I don't know how long we're staying here, but I'd like to part a little beaver before we go, Butterfly." He looked hopefully at the big woman.

But she shook her head and pointed at her 'girls'. "There you are. Pay and take your choice. I'm off outside to see what's going on." With that she was gone, leaving them to stare at that delightful rump swinging side to side under the thin material like clockwork . . .

Zander smoked one of the captured *Camels*, while in the corner of the room, Grimm gorged himself on chocolate as if he were back in his schooldays, making little sounds of delight and muttering to himself, "Oh, this piece has got nuts in it . . . this one's fudge."

The two SS officers ignored the civilian as they planned the next stage of their mission, staring at the map spread out on the table between them.

"Up to last month," Zander explained. "Most of the *Ami* supplies were coming up to the front by road. The Red Ball Express, the Amis called it, run day and night, mostly by blacks like those we've just captured. But now the Americans have opened up Marseilles and Cherbourg so that their supply ships can run into those ports and have patched up the French State Railway System, so they're beginning to use rail to bring up supplies for the front to railheads on the western side of the Vosges. From there they are transported the rest of the way by these black truckers of the Red Ball Express. *Klar*, Kuno?"

"Yes, very clear, Heinz. But what have the railways got to do with us?"

Zander ignored the question. Instead, with his one hand he traced a line on the map. "Now we're roughly here – not far from Ste Marie-aux-Mines. Once we're passed it and through the high pass beyond, the Vosges start to give way to the foothills where St Die – here – is situated." He let von Dodenburg follow the route he was indicating, before adding, "And at St Die there is a small American marshalling yard."

Von Dodenburg looked at the SS General curiously, wondering what all this was leading to. Outside in the street, they had locked away the surviving blacks in the local Gendarmerie jail. Now the street was empty save for the dead, the still burning tank, and a tall impressive woman, who walked slowly despite the cold and the dead sprawled everywhere, just as if she were out for a stroll. He frowned. Somebody ought to make her move off the street.

Zander stubbed out his cigarette with an air of finality. "Tomorrow morning at dawn, when the *Amis* and the French will be fast asleep, we are going to attack that marshalling yard, Kuno," he announced.

"Attack it!" von Dodenburg echoed, caught completely off guard by the statement.

"Yes, tomorrow we're going to change our mode of transport." Zander grinned at the look of surprise on the younger man's face.

"But how?"

"Easy – we're going to steal a train, Kuno . . ."

* * *

Outside, Butterfly saw the young SS officer watching her. She decided it was time to move on. Thoughtfully she started down the street, eyes not even taking in the dead sprawled out in the grotesque postures of those done violently to death. Since 1936 when Franco had attacked the Republic she had seen enough dead men. She had become used to them, but sick of them. Spaniards, Moors, English, French, German, American, all dead for some foolish cause or other, dead before they had begun to live.

For four long years during the Occupation she had saved the money her 'girls' had earned her. Now it was worthless and she had begun to start all over again. For she was sick of men and sex. She wanted that farm in the Jura badly, but she needed money to buy it.

Her pace quickened as she turned down the side alley where Jo-Jo had his rundown workshop. He was a dirty treacherous little runt, but he was her contact with 'Colonel Hugo' and his band. For a month now, ever since the Americans had come into the Vosges she had been using Jo-Jo to pass on information about the US convoys running in and out of St Die. The blacks, naïve and flattered by her attention as they were, never could keep a secret with her.

If the US convoy was small enough and the trucks contained something that could be sold on the black market, such as petrol or blankets, Colonel Hugo and his outlaws attacked it. She had received a part of the proceedings. But again it was in, what were virtually worthless, French francs. But what were these Germans carrying with them? She bit her bottom lip in bewilderment.

Jo-Jo was, as usual, working at his *gazogene*, a battered pre-war Renault with a huge bag of coal gas on its roof, which powered the vehicle in lieu of petrol, and as usual he had a cheap cigarette glued to the bottom lip of his ratlike face. "*Salut,*" she said, as she stopped at the open door of the cluttered workshop.

"*Salut,*" he replied hoarsely, not stopping his tinkering.

"I'd like you to take a message to Colonel Hugo," she said softly.

He dropped his spanner and turned to face her. "You know it's getting dangerous. The Americans are beginning to patrol the pass with armed white mice." He meant the white-helmeted military policemen.

"Life's dangerous," she replied drily. "Besides there's money in it for you, Jo-Jo."

"What good's money these days?" he said. "It can't buy much." He eyed her splendid breasts greedily.

"So that's it, eh," she said. "All right, but you know my way."

"I got a sofa at the back. You'd be more comfortable on that, Butterfly."

She shook her head firmly. "No my way or not at all."

"But that way makes my knees tremble, Butterfly."

She ignored his remark. "Make up your mind, Jo-Jo."

"All right," he said and started to fumble with his flies, while she lowered her knickers and drew up the front of her skirt to reveal sturdy shapely thighs surmounted by a thick tuft of jet-black hair.

"Come on then, don't take all day. Stick it in me and for God's sake take off that cap before you start anything."

Hastily he did so and then thrust himself into her, panting and groaning already, while she stared in silent boredom at the flaking ceiling.

Five minutes later, it was all over and complaining

that, "my knees are trembling like jelly," he was on his way to the pass in the ancient vehicle, while she stared after it telling herself that Jo-Jo was a "salaud". But then she concluded all men were.

Chapter Five

It was snowing hard when they set off again just after midnight and for once they were glad of the snow. They reasoned that the new snow might keep American patrols off the roads until the weather improved. Behind them they left Negroes kocked up in the little jail and had warned the civilians not to attempt to let them out till morning. To make quite sure von Dodenburg had retained the jail's keys, throwing them away when they were well outside the little hamlet.

Now at a steady ten kilometres an hour, they crept round the mining village of Ste Marie-aux-Mines and began the stiff climb that led out of the place on the road to St Die.

Up in the front truck, taken from the black soldiers, with the windscreen wipers ticking back and forth noisely, Zander explained a little more of his pain. "Intelligence in Berlin informed me that there is a daily mail train that arrives at the outskirts of the marshalling yards at St Die. It is called the 'V-Mail Express'."

"V-Mail Express?" von Dodenburg queried.

"Intelligence says that it is the name given to the US Forces' airmail letter. Well, this Express is only a small train – a locomotive and five or six coaches in which the mail is roughly sorted during the trip from Cherbourg. Then in St Die at the main sorting office, another crew sorts the letters more precisely. So we are dealing with a bunch of clerks really and a couple of French crewmen who man the locomotive."

"They might have armed guards on board like we do on all troop trains, Heinz."

Zander grinned in the green glowing darkness of the cab. "No one in his right mind is going to desert from a cushy job like that, I should think, Kuno. It's ten times better than the fighting front."

Von Dodenburg returned his grin and said, "I suppose you're right, Heinz."

"Now the beauty of the postal business is that the V-Mail Express's depot is away from the main lines where the troop trains and the like will be."

Von Dodenburg nodded his understanding. "I take your point, Heinz. If we play it carefully and nobble them without alerting the rest of the marshalling yard, we can be on our way—" He stopped short and added, puzzled again. "To where?"

"You'll learn in due course, Kuno. He patient. So far only I and that horned ox of a civilian, Grimm, know our destination. I think it's better that way in case any of our people get captured and are forced to talk."

"I suppose, you're right, Heinz," von Dodenburg conceded. "But won't the *Amis* miss the train and soon stop us on our way to wherever we're going?"

"I've thought about that. So we've got to take the American postal crew with us, leaving with them at the V-Mail Express's usual departure time, as if we were going back to Cherbourg, which we aren't, to pick up a fresh supply of mail for the front. With a bit of luck on our side, I think we should be able to pull it off, Kuno."

"I suppose so," von Dodenburg said without his usual enthusiasm.

Then the two of them lapsed into silence, lulled into a kind of half doze by the steady to and fro of the windscreen wipers as the truck ground its way up the steep incline. But von Dodenburg's mind was still working, as he sat there, eyes closed. He was puzzled and worried. What were they doing, he asked himself, dressed in American uniform in the middle of France? He already knew they would be shot out of hand if they were captured and his first duty was to his brave troopers who were prepared to take the risk of being executed because they were loyal to him.

Could he still continue with this mysterious mission on that basis? He frowned in the darkness and thought to himself, if only I knew in three devils' name what the mission is. Damnit!

The convoy rolled on through the snow.

Colonel Hugo, muffled up in his dyed American greatcoat, a thick woollen scarf wrapped around his ears, wiped the snowflakes from his plump face for the umpteenth time and told himself he was a fool to be out in this kind of weather at his age. But still the whore's tip was good. The Boche, dressed as Americans, must be carrying something very precious to take such risks. The rats were leaving the sinking ship obviously. Were they taking their treasure with them? He guessed they might be.

Once Colonel Hugo had been a member of the hated Vichy* *milice* working together with the German hunting down Jews, Maquisards and similar rats. But when the war had started to turn against the Germans, Colonel Hugo had realized that his life was in danger once the Allies won.

* The wartime pro-German French government.

Almost overnight he had transformed himself into a Maquis leader. But after the Liberation there had been little for him to do save join the new French Army, but that would have meant risking his life once more for a pittance.

So he had turned bandit, ambushing small American convoys and selling the loot on the black market in the big French cities in the rear.

Hijacking lone American trucks, usually manned by those "niggers", as he called them, whom he hated with a passion, was relatively without risk and the proceeds from the hijacks allowed him to live a good life with a string of mistresses and as much good cognac as he could drink.

Still Colonel Hugo was clever enough to realize that he couldn't last as a bandit for much longer up here in these freezing, snowbound mountains. Already in the last week he and his gang had been forced to dodge patrols of US military police in jeeps.

Soon the Americans would organize a proper sweep through the hills for his hiding place and he knew his rabble of *Milice*, deserters from the French Army and petty criminals wouldn't last long against regular US troops. He had to make the big killing before then and 'go underground' in one of the big cities to the rear of the front.

He shivered again. Around him in the rocks his men were doing the same and he could hear the faint clink of bottles, as they tried to ward off the freezing cold with cheap cognac or the like. He pulled a face. They were indeed a rabble, but surprise would be on their side and that would mean a successful attack.

Colonel Hugo looked again at the dial of his wristwatch. Nearly two. Butterfly's go-between, Jo-Jo, had said the Americans would be leaving just after midnight so it might take them another quarter of an hour to reach this spot. It was time to start making preparations for the ambush. He turned and snapped, "All right put out the tyre-busters. You and you – and you – clear the snow. The rest of you put the stoppers in place."

"Yes Colonel," they answered dutifully, though all of them knew that the highest rank he had ever achieved had been that of a corporal in the *Milice*. Three men with brooms started to sweep away the snow, while others placed ugly-looking iron spikes in the cleared spaces. Hugo nodded his approval. Those spikes, once used by the *Milice* at road blocks when they were hunting the Maquis, would penetrate the thickest of tyres. The damned Boche *would* be in for a surprise.

Then he closed his eyes and, trying to forgot the biting cold, thought of how his current mistress, a convent-educated virgin of eighteen a short time before, had taken it in her mouth and had sucked it slowly and gently for what seemed an eternity; and how she had actually thanked him afterwards for allowing her the 'great pleasure' of having done so. He smiled softly to himself and told himself that there were certain sexual advantages of having a girl who was innocent . . .

In the second truck Schulze couldn't sleep like the rest of the Wotan troopers snoring all around him in the back. He wriggled back and forth and next to him Matz said sleepily, "Can't you pack it up, Schulzi. Yer frigging wriggling around like some frigging bitch on heat."

"You'll be frigging wriggling around at the end of my fist in half a mo," Schulze snorted back. "I want a piss badly. My frigging bladder's busting."

"Well, let it bust," Matz answered unkindly. "I want to get some sack-time in."

"You call yersen a friend," Schulze said. "Yer know I need help when I try to piss over the side. Somebody's got to hold the funnel cos I need both hands to raise the thing I've got between my legs. It's not all shriven up like that poor little bit of gristle you've got down there. How you can ever satisfy a woman with that that docked-off dick, I'll never know—"

"Oh come on, let's get it over," Matz interrupted him impatiently. "I'll get the funnel. You get to the side."

Matz thrust the funnel, used for filling oil into engines, down the side of the truck between the metal side and the tarpaulin. Meanwhile Schulze had opened his flies and with a great lot of grunting and panting, he had pulled out his penis.

"Stop making a frigging production out of it," Matz urged.

"Well, you would if you had a dong as big as mine. It weighs something. Why do you think I've got them round shoulders."

"Get on with it."

While Matz held the funnel in place, Schulze hung on to a stanchion to steady himself and inserted his penis into the funnel.

"Don't frigging well splash me," Matz warned.

Schulze gave a great sigh of relief as the urine started to flow in a noisy hot, steaming rush. "Wonderful to get that off my chest," he exclaimed in delight.

"Watch where yer pissing," Matz snorted. "You just pissed on my flipper. I don't know what you've got. I might end up with a withered hand or something. The things you've stuck yer salami into, yer could have all sorts of horrible diseases, for all I know."

"Aw go and crap in yer cap," Schulze began. "What's a little piss between friends—" He stopped short suddenly, urination finished but with his penis still stuck in the funnel.

"What's up?" Matz asked in sudden alarm.

"Look at that at ten o'clock!" Schulze replied urgently. "Can you see through the snow?"

"Holy mackerel," Matz, who had the keenest eyes in the whole of Wotan, exclaimed, as he spotted the light blinking on and off, red against the white of the falling snow. "Someone's signalling out there."

"Yes," Schulze agreed, "and they're frigging well signalling we're coming . . ."

Chapter Six

"*Bande de salauds!*" Colonel Hugo cursed, his teeth chattering with cold as he did so. "Where are they?"

Patrick, the deserter from the Ist French Army in the Vosges, who acted as his second-in-command, said, "Well, Colonel, it's a good hour since we saw the signal from down there where the lookout is posted. Has something gone wrong?"

"How in heaven's name should I know," Hugo rounded on him angrily. "They should have been here by now. Those damned Boche have always been unreliable. They pride themselves on their efficiency." He puffed out his fat cheeks with contempt. "They don't even know the meaning of the word. Only we French have a system that works."

Patrick said nothing. Nominally he was French, but he thought of himself as an Alsatian German. He had no great opinion of the French.

Hugo looked at his watch again. "All right," he decided, "let us break our own rules and signal the lookout. The Boche will be too stupid to notice on a night like this. And get those rogues of ours to clear the snow away from the tyre-busters they're covered with the stuff again."

"*Oui, Mon Colonel,*" Patrick said, as if he were back in the regular army and then he actually saluted.

Hugo was flattered, but at the same time suspicious. Was Patrick trying to make a fool of him? Then he dismissed the thought and concentrated on staring down the height, as the man next to him raised his signal lantern and began to flash it off and on.

Minutes passed and there was no answer.

"*Sale con*!" Colonel Hugo cursed out loud. "What's the matter with the man, has he gone to sleep?"

The signaller tried again and this time there was a reply. Down the height, there came a flash of green. That meant the coast was clear. A moment later the green light changed to red, which meant danger was approaching: the Boche were coming!

Colonel Hugo rapped out an order. The men scrambled for the rocks and took up their firing positions once more, as from below there came the faint sound of a motor engine labouring its way up the steep incline. Hugo allowed himself a faint smile. "They're coming," he hissed to the men closest. "Now we've got them. They're walking straight into a trap."

The Germans slid through the bushes, grateful for the mountain wind which dislodged the snow from the branches of the firs and muffled their approach in regular flurries of falling snow. Carefully they worked their way up the rough path that led to the pass. There were ten of them, led by Schulze and Matz, all armed to the teeth, with bags of captured American egg grenades slung around their necks.

"There are not a lot of you," von Dodenburg had announced just before they had left, "but you've got surprise on your side. And Schulze," he had warned, "take no risks. I want all of them back."

Schulze in reply had lifted one massive thigh and ripped

off a tremendous fart, saying, "Don't you be worrying, sir. I could tackle that lot of frogs up there with one hand tied behind me back mesen. After all yer can't say much for people who make love with their tongues. So I'll just take these cardboard soldiers with me for a bit of company. Come on, young gentlemen, Uncle Schulze is gonna take yer for a little stroll in the moonlight."

Now the minutes passed slowly as they drew closer to the pass. Faintly they could hear the sound of the single truck, the decoy, grinding its way up the heights. When they were a hundred metres away from the summit, Schulze whispered for them to leave the rough track. They couldn't chance bumping into any sentry that the 'frog bandits', as he called them, might have posted there. They started to plod through the knee-deep snow, making what Schulze thought was one hell of a noise, but he knew there was no other way.

Suddenly Matz grabbed his arm. "What is it, apeturd?" Schulze hissed.

"Can't you smell it?"

"The only thing I can smell is you, you Bavarian barnshitter," Schulze growled.

"*Sniff*!" Matz urged. "Use yer frigging hooter."

Schulze did so. He caught a whiff of pungent French cigarette smoke on the keen mountain air. He nodded. "I see what you mean. They're up there in the rocks, Matzi."

"Yer, God knows what you'd do, you big ape, without me. Come on, let's get the bastards before they spot us."

Now Colonel Huge could see the dark outline of the big truck, as it laboured its way up the slope, churning up the new snow, but pushing on deliberately. "One hundred metres at the most," he said to himself, calculating that was the distance between it and the line of tyre-busters which had been placed across the mountain road. "*Allez*," he alerted the men, cocking his own sten gun and resting it on the rock in front of him.

Obediently they carried out Colonel Hugo's order, watching fascinated as the first truck continued to drive straight into the trap they had set for it, each man already wondering what he would do with the loot, knowing however that most of it would go to pay for the raddled favours of the Butterfly's whores.

Now the truck was almost upon them. The ambushers tensed. In a minute its front tyres would hit the tyre-busters. Idly Colonel Hugo wondered about the other trucks that JoJo had told them about. Still one alone might contain all the treasure they would need.

"*Now!*" he yelled in the very same instant that the truck's front tyres ran over the spikes. They exploded as one. Crazily the truck slewed to one side, its bonnet slamming into the rock face, as a hail of fire slashed its tarpaulin to ribbons.

The air was suddenly full of the cloying stench of escaping petrol as the wrecked truck's engine spluttered and died.

"Come on, men," Colonel Hugo yelled exuberantly. "We've got them. There's no answering fire. Let's see what they've got."

Fifty metres away, Matz thrust his hand over the surprised sentry's mouth to prevent him from yelling out, and in that very same instant, he slid his trench knife into his back. The sentry's spine arched like a taut bowstring. Next moment Matz released his grip and he slumped to the snow, moaning softly as he died. The way ahead was clear.

As Colonel Hugo's men streamed forward to loot the wrecked truck, Schulze's group tensed among the rocks they had just abandoned. "All right," Schulze commanded, "let the treacherous arseholes have it." He raised his machine pistol and pressed the trigger. The automatic burst into frenetic life. Slugs sliced the night air. Men went down on all sides, caught by surprise, galvanized into the sudden action like puppets at the behest of a crazy puppet master.

At Schulze's side, Matz pulled out the cotter pin of an egg grenade with his front teeth and flung at the looters, crying, "Try that frigging one for size, frogs!"

The grenade exploded in a burst of angry violet light. The looters reeled back, holding their shattered faces, with the Alsatian, Patrick, moaning in his thick Alsatian German, "*Ich bin blind* . . . Someone help me, please God, *I'm blind*!" But on that terrible night of treachery and double treachery God was looking the other way.

Now Schulze's group was pouring a steady fire into the looters, who were trapped on the road, hemmed in by the rock wall on the far side where the wrecked truck lay. Some tried desperately to clamber up the rock wall, fighting for holds to lever themselves upwards. To no avail. Schulze's troopers shot them down mercilessly and they fell screaming to the road, dead before they hit the tarmac.

In the end, with the road littered with the bodies of the dead and dying, the survivors tried to surrender. But Schulze knew they couldn't be burdened with prisoners, especially a treacherous bunch like these mountain bandits, who would have shown no mercy to them if the roles had been reversed.

"No prisoners!" he ordered grimly and shot a survivor who had gone down on his knees, wringing his hands in the classic pose of supplication, tears streaming down his ashen face.

Schulze's troopers needed no urging. One by one they shot the survivors till not one of them was left standing. Then it was all over, and the shooting died away, leaving behind it a loud echoing silence which seemed to go on for ever.

"All right," Schulze commanded. "Let's get the truck out of the way. I can hear the others coming now."

Clinging to the underside of the wrecked truck, Colonel Hugo prayed fervently, as he had never prayed since he had been a frightened schoolboy. *Oh Good Lord, don't let them find me! Please good Lord help me in my hour of need* . . . His prayer ended in a gasp, as strong hands took hold of the truck and sent it rolling into the drainage ditch at the side of the road. Petrol poured over his upturned face and made him choke and gasp. But nothing else happened. Thus he lay there, tears of joy trickling down his fat face. He had been saved.

Up on the road, Zander slapped Schulze heartily on the back and said, "*Gut gemacht, Schulze.* Well done, you've saved our bacon again. If you hadn't have spotted that light and Matz here hadn't suggested the decoy truck, with the stake jammed over the accelerator, I don't think we could have gotten through this pass so easily. A man and a boy could have held it for an eternity." He looked at the dead Frenchmen without interest. "Well, they didn't make it, did they, Kuno?" he said, turning away from a beaming Schulze to von Dodenburg.

The latter did not share the General's enthusiasm. He said, "One thing is clear, Heinz, somebody in the village down there let these bandits or whatever they are, know we were coming. The question now is – how many others know what we're about?"

Standartenführer Zander answered, "Now, Kuno, don't go broody on me. We're almost there, you know. A couple of hours more and with a bit of luck we'll be in St Die."

Under the truck in the drainage ditch, Colonel Hugo didn't understand much of the German being used by the two officers, but he did hear the name of the town quite clearly. *St Die*, he thought to himself, so that's where they're heading. From there? He shrugged and didn't attempt to answer his own question. Let them get off first and once he was in safety, he would see what advantage he could make of that particular piece of information.

"I suppose you're right, Heinz," von Dodenburg agreed.

"Of course I am, old house. Let's get on with it. The snow's stopped. I think we can up our speed a little." Zander turned and called, "All right, troopers – mount up."

"Roll 'em," von Dodenburg yelled.

Moments later they were on their way again, leaving a shivering Colonel Hugo planning his revenge.

Chapter Seven

"You wanna a jig-jig?" the whore asked, as she lounged there in the doorway. It was barely light and she made her offer clear by holding a flashlight to her loins and illuminating her crotch, as she spread her legs. It was obvious she wasn't wearing knickers beneath her thin dress. "I cheap. Five dollars for fuck."

Zander shook his head and von Dodenburg who understood English said swiftly, "Got to go to work, *cherie*."

She shrugged and dismissed them, as they set off again down the *Rue de Gare*, which led to the sidings where the mail train was located.

"Heaven, arse and cloudburst," Zander exploded when they were out of earshot. "Those damned Americans must have some stamina. Whores offering to get rid of their dirty water for them at this time of the morning. And in this cold!" He shivered dramatically.

Von Dodenburg chuckled. "As Schulze, the big rogue, would say, the pleasures of the common soldier are rare and few."

Zander chuckled, too, despite the tension which gripped the two of them. They knew that they wouldn't last long if they were stopped by enemy military policemen. They had no papers and von Dodenburg's English was only rudimentary. They had to find the V-Mail Express and take it swiftly. Already French workers on bicycles, cigarettes glued to their lips, baguettes under their arms, were going to work. Soon the whole of St Die would be on its feet. Time was running out fast.

Von Dodenburg turned and looked up and down the street. It looked pretty safe in the grey light of the new dawn. He whistled shrilly. The first truck nudged its way around the corner. He jerked his clenched fist up and down three times, the infantry signal for hurry it up. Matz at the wheel flung it in second gear and the truck moved faster. Behind it the second one appeared. In the back of both trucks, hidden by the tarpaulin, there were heavily armed troopers of Wotan, ready for action, but von Dodenburg hoped it wouldn't come to that. He nodded his approval. The two officers walked on.

Now they could see the marshalling yards. They were a big complex, packed with locomotives and carriages, though at the moment only the little stubby shunting engines were moving, pulling carriages to and fro in readiness for the day's traffic.

Trying to appear like two soldiers reluctantly setting off for another morning's hard boring work, Zander and von Dodenburg surveyed the yard with the keen gaze of professional soldiers, looking for potential danger spots.

They could make out a guard post on the platform of the main station, next to what they took to be the RTO's* office, which was manned by white-helmeted American military policeman. There were a couple of French gendarmes in capes, with dogs walking the various tracks. Probably they were checking that no attempt was being made to break into the rolling stock

---

* Railway Transport Officer.

which contained supplies for the front. They looked bored and uninterested and Zander commented, "What do you think, Kuno? It looks all right to me."

"Me, too."

"Shall we find the postal train?"

"I think it's safe."

Behind them the trucks continued to crawl down the Rue de Gare. To any casual observer they looked just like another small American convoy, waiting to haul supplies from the marshalling yard. Von Dodenburg placed his outstretched fingers on the top of his helmet. Again it was an infantry signal. This time it meant close up on me.

They passed a café. For that time of the day it was loud with music, noise and harsh brittle laughter. Cigarette smoke poured from it and there was the stink of stale beer. In the doorway, a dyed blonde was cuddled up to a drunken American, her hand inside his flies. Neither she nor he seemed to notice the two strangers; they were too busy at what they were doing. Zander shook his head in mock wonder. Behind them the GI started to gasp, "I'm coming . . . *Goddammit, I'm coming*!"

Von Dodenburg grinned at the gasped words. "Nice start for a cold frosty morning," he commented.

Behind them in the leading truck, Schulze saw the whore and the soldier and said enviously, "That's better than a mug of nigger sweat any day. Sets a poor common soldier up for the rest of the day, Matzi."

"You should know, you old beaver-basher," Matz answered sourly. "Now keep yer frigging glassy orbits on the C.O., will yer. This place is lousy with *Amis*. Anything can happen."

"All right, all right," Schulze said patiently, "don't

have yer monthlies." All the same he took his gaze off the couple sagging now in the doorway.

In front von Dodenburg and Zander walked casually to the little mail train. There was a stove pipe protruding from the boarded up windows of the middle coach and there was a trail of thin blue smoke coming from it. So they knew that there was already somebody on board. Otherwise they couldn't see any sign of other occupants. "Wonder where they are?" Zander asked softly.

"Probably over there in that café-cum-brothel. But they should be reporting for work soon, if your intelligence is correct."

"'Spect you're right," Zander agreed, as two civilians with railwaymen's caps came into sight, carrying little tin pails, muffled up to the eyes in scarves in the French fashion.

Zander nodded and the bigger of the two looked up from checking the time with his watch and nodded, giving him a grumpy "*M'sieu*".

They clambered aboard the locomotive.

Out of the side of his mouth, Zander whispered, "Intelligence was right. Things are beginning to move."

"*Drunk last night, drunk the night before, gonna get drunk tonight like I never get drunk before . . .*"

Zander and von Dodenburg swung round startled.

A fat postal clerk with his cap on the back of his shaven head, was weaving from side to side as he emerged from the café, with behind him comrades crying, "Knock it off, Hymen. You'll have the goddam MPs on to us!"

The fat soldier waved his cognac bottle at them and said, "Fuck the MPs . . . *All good friend, jolly good company,*" he continued to warble as he fell up the little metal steps into the first coach.

"The clerks," Zander whispered as the postal workers,

111

most of them drunk, followed the fat one inside. "Things *are* beginning to move."

Behind them the trucks came to a halt. Zander and von Dodenburg waited impatiently. Were there any more clerks to come?

Up ahead at the locomotive they could hear the scrape of a shovel on coal, as the fireman started to stoke the boiler. A bent-shouldered railwayman, carrying a large hammer, was now going from wheel to wheel, tapping it and listening for any defects. Soon the train would be setting off on its return journey to the port of Cherbourg.

Von Dodenburg whistled.

Schulze dropped to the ground, followed by half a dozen Wotan troopers. All of them carried sticks in their hands. Von Dodenburg indicated the train. Schulze nodded his understanding.

The wheel-tapper saw the men armed with sticks. He looked at them for a moment, then got on with his job. Everyone knew Americans were crazy, he told himself. Moments later he started to cross the lines to commence work on another train.

Up at the locomotive, the driver had fired the boiler. Steam was streaming into the cold dawn sky. There was the hiss of more steam escaping from near the pistons. The time had come to move, von Dodenburg knew that. He flung a last glance around the yard. No one seemed to be taking any notice of them. Oh the platform the MPs next to the RTO's office were looking bored, as if they couldn't wait for their shift to end. "All right, Schulze," he commanded, "go to it."

Schulze lifted a fist like a small steam shovel and grinned. "*Zu Befehl, Obersturmbannführer,*" he answered with excessive military politeness.

"*Verpiss dich,*" von Dodenburg answered crudely.

Schulze's grin broadened even more. He pushed by the two officers, followed by the raiding party. In his mind, he was already downing that bottle of cognac he had seen in the fat clerk's pudgy hand. There might be more booze stashed away on the train, too. He licked his big lips in anticipation and swung himself up into the first coach.

It was empty. Obviously it was the sorting coach, for there were little pigeon holes set along the walls and on the floor there were empty sacks and pieces of twine with which the sorters tied up the packets of letters.

Schulze beckoned for the others to follow him.

They moved into the second coach. The clerks sprawled on their bunks, some already in their underwear, others busy pulling off their clothes and making ready to crawl under the rough brown blankets. There was a stink of sweaty feet and stale tobacco smoke. Someone was saying, "I'm sorry, fellahs, I think I'm gonna be sick—". He stopped short when he saw the gigantic man filling the door frame, a club in his hand, his sickness forgotten immediately. "Hey, guy what you're doing here?" This place is strictly off limits—" Schulze leaned over and tapped him on the back of his crewcut. The man went out like a light, eyes crossed, all thoughts of vomiting now gone.

The clerks looked alarmed. The fat one with the cognac bottle stared open-mouthed at the giant, bottle suspended in his hand in midair, as if he were about to take a slug from it.

In sudden alarm Schulze grabbed it from him, snarling, "Drop that firewater, arse-with-ears, and it'll be the last move you'll ever make."

The fat clerk didn't understand German, but he

recognized the threatening tone. "Don't hit me!" he quavered. "Please, I'm not a well man."

Now they worked their way progressively through the little train, taking the handful of clerks prisoners until they came to the last coach. On the door was a sign stating, '*O/C Train. Knock and Wait to Enter*'.

A young trooper who had learnt some basic English at school, translated the sign for Schulze and the latter chortled, as he heard the rythmic sound of bed springs squeaking from inside the coach. "I'll *knock* on his frigging face. He's probably practising a bit of the old one-hand widow by the sound of it."

He flung open the door violently and found to his surprise that for once he was wrong.

'The O/C Train' was certainly not playing with himself.

"By the Great Wizard and all His Triangles," Schulze exploded – when he saw the cause of the noise. "What a way to go!"

A very small white man was submerged by the huge bulk of a coloured woman, naked save for sheer white silk stockings, who was pumping herself up and down relentlessly on the 'O/C Train', the sweat pouring down her gleaming brown body, while the little man whimpered with either pain or pleasure, for it was was hard to tell, then his face was submerged beneath her great breasts.

Schulze swallowed hard as that huge rump went up and down, up and down, totally unaware that she had spectators now. "That moves me, comrades," he said thickly. "Gives me a lump in me throat to see something kind and good in this cruel old world."

"It's not in me throat where *I* get a lump," one of the troopers chortled as the little man sank ever deeper into the mattress under that enormous weight.

Schulze shook his head as if he no longer understood the world. "You young fellers don't have one bit of romance in yer. That's beautiful that is. A performance like that deserves a round of applause, you ignorant piece of apeturd. What a lot of primitives." He shook his head once again.

Up front, Zander and von Dodenburg strolled, apparently casually, towards the locomotive. They could hear the noise of the fireman shovelling coal and the roar of the flames coming out of the open firebox. They stopped at the side of the tender. The driver took no notice of them. He was too busy checking the steam pressure and other technical matters. But the fireman did. He looked down at them said in broken English, "What you want, GI. Forbidden," he wagged a finger at them. "*Interdit.*"

Von Dodenburg pretended not to notice. He started to climb the ladder to the cab. The fireman swung his shovel. Von Dodenburg ducked. The big shovel hit the side of the cab. His brawny arms trembled with the impact. Von Dodenburg didn't give him a chance to recover. He jammed his pistol into the man's ribs and said in his best French, "*Travail, tu salaud!*"

The fireman's mouth dropped open with surprise. But he obeyed all right. He worked.

Five minutes later they were pulling away, apparently on schedule, for the RTO, with his important-looking check board, checked them off and then waved. Seconds later they were working their way round a curve and St Die started to disappear. They were on their way again. Where, von Dodenburg did not know, but somehow he felt it was going to be somewhere unpleasant.

Part Three

THE FLEMING PLOY

Chapter One

"We've got another clue," Fleming said thoughtfully, as he entered the little HQ, where Captain Hurd and Mrs Smith were sitting enjoying another mug of 'sarnt-major's tea' brought in by Corporal White. Outside, despite the freezing fog that shrouded the sea, they could hear the sound of gunfire. The Americans besieging Lorient were obviously trying another local counterattack, thinking that the German defenders wouldn't expect them to do so in such weather.

Mrs Smith smiled politely, but said nothing. Hurd, for his part, put down his mug hastily and said, "Fire away, Commander. I'm all ears."

Commander Fleming gave him that sardonic smile of his and said, "Well, hear this then. I've just had a call from British Military Intelligence at Shaef in Paris," Fleming meant Allied Supreme Headquarters, "and they've got a hold of a Maquis chap, named Colonel Hugo or something. All these partisans give themselves grandiose military titles. Anyway this fellow reports that he attempted to attack a small convoy of trucks in the High Vosges. He failed and he was the only one of his group to survive."

"But what were Germans doing in the High Vosges?" Hurd objected. "Those mountains have been in Allied hands since last month."

"Exactly," Fleming agreed and, lighting a cigarette, placed it in the ivory holder he affected. "And these Germans were in *American* uniforms."

For the first time Mrs Smith's face showed some animation. "You think that these Germans have something to do with the Japanese submarine at Lorient." With a nod of her head she indicated the fog-shrouded enemy port.

"Yes, especially as this Colonel Hugo chap swears that the Germans belonged to the SS. He heard one of them using SS ranks which are different to those of the German Army. In fact, he says that the rank in question was *Standartenführer*, which is the equivalent—"

"Of a general," she beat him to it with a faint smile.

"You speak German?"

She shrugged slightly. "I studied at the University of Berlin for a year in 1935."

Fleming warmed to Mrs Smith even more. She wasn't in the least 'beddable', as he would have phrased it, but she was pretty damn smart. "So," he continued, "what is an SS general doing, leading a small convoy of trucks way behind the American lines?" He paused and let his question sink in.

Out to sea, scarlet flashes stabbed the grey gloom and there was the hollow boom of heavy artillery rolling in over the water. Obviously the Americans were using a warship to support their attack. Perhaps Fleming told himself that this was the first phase of an all-out American attack. Perhaps he need not worry any longer about the Jap sub and whatever its cargo was.

Then he remembered how the American losses had totalled ten thousand at Brest before they had been able to take the port and reasoned that the US Army couldn't afford another all-out attack like that. No this would be just a local affair after all. They still had the problem of the Jap sub on their hands.

"And what happened to these disguised Jerries?" Hurd asked.

"Our informant, this Colonel Hugo chappie, swears he heard them say they were heading for the little town of St Die to the west of the High Vosges."

"And?" Hurd demanded.

"Well, if they got there no one has yet spotted them. At the present time Com Z, that's the Yanks' communications and supply service behind the lines, has ordered all MP units in the area to search for them." He shrugged. "So far without any luck."

His announcement was followed by several minutes of silence while all three of them ran the matter through their minds. Outside the counterfire from the German land-based batteries had commenced. Great jets of water were hurtling into the sky around the lean grey shape of the American warship. But the American skipper was out-thinking the German gunners, scurrying back and forth at speed. Soon, Fleming guessed, he'd make smoke and disappear while the going was good.

"It would seem to me," Mrs Smith said slowly breaking the brooding silence inside the little HQ, "that by now these American MPs would have found the Germans' trucks."

"My thinking, too," Fleming said quickly. "Apparently, as soon as the Maquis colonel told them what he knew, they put up road blocks everywhere to a depth of fifty miles from St Die – and in this kind of weather, the German trucks couldn't cover much more than that in a whole day."

Mrs Smith nodded. "So can we conclude that they abandoned the trucks and found some other means of transportation for their journey to Lorient, if that is where they are heading?"

Hurd grinned at the professorial manner in which Mrs Smith had made her statement. But at the same time, he admired her. The woman obviously was as sharp as a razor.

Fleming clicked his fingers with excitement. "Exactly. The Huns knew they'd be rumbled some time or other, so they abandoned the trucks and found some other way of getting here." His eyes blazed. "And I'm nearly one hundred percent sure they're coming this way. Why else would an SS general be involved in an operation which might end up with all of them being shot as spies because they're dressed in American uniforms? It's got to be them."

"I'm inclined to agree," Hurd said thoughtfully. "First the Japs – er – Japanese are risking a very valuable submarine. Then there is this SS general involved. Commander I'm sure the two go together. But what the hell is so damned important for them to take such risks?"

"Would it not be better," Mrs Smith said softly, "to consider what mode of transport they are using now and how we might be able to apprehend these Germans before they get to Lorient with whatever is so important?"

"A good point, Mrs Smith. I feel like a schoolkid again at Eton being put on the right course by some beak."

Mrs Smith smiled but said nothing.

"They've got to cover – perhaps – couple of hundred miles from St Die to here. Then they're got to get through the Yanks' lines around Lorient which wouldn't be easy. So what kind of transport could they use to do that?"

"I would suggest a train," Mrs Smith said baldly.

Outside the American warship was making smoke and the gunfire at sea and on land was beginning to die away.

It was obvious that the American attack had failed or was being broken off due to casualties. As always Lorient was proving a tough nut to crack.

"*A train*," Fleming echoed, face revealing his astonishment at her remark. "But how?"

"Steal one. Trucks stolen, either military or civilian, would be noticed soon enough and reported to the authorities. But it would be different with a train, especially in wartime with many trains being run under the authority of the military and no longer sticking to the regular timetables of the civilian railway authorities. Indeed, I suspect, the military don't want the civilians to know much about such matters because of security and sabotage."

"I take your point," Flaming said slowly and thoughtfully. "But to steal a train – that's a tall order, Mrs Smith."

She didn't respond and Fleming added, "All right, let us say a train is the means of transportation they are using to get to Lorient. They'll have to get off it somewhere before Lorient because no train naturally goes through the Yanks' front line in to the besieged port. So where would they get off and how would they get their cargo through the front line and into Lorient?"

"That's one hell of a lot of questions, Commander," Hurd said. "But if they're coming from the general direction of St Die, they'd use the line to Epinal – look here." He strode over to the large map of France on the wall opposite. "From there they'd obviously go south of Paris because in the capital all the main lines end at one or other of the great stations, as you know, Fleming."

The Commander nodded.

"Then it would be Le Mans, perhaps to Rennes and Josselin, here, and that would be about it. Josselin would be about the end of the line for them. He faltered to a stop. "Christ, one really needs a crystal ball to solve this one."

"A crystal ball?" Mrs Smith echoed puzzled.

"Yes," Hurd replied, "so one could see into the future."

"All right," Fleming made up his mind, "we'll alert the Com Z authorities to make special checks at the stations you mentioned for anything unusual. Then I suggest you take another team into Lorient. We've got to find out whether the Japanese are making any preparations for departure now. That would help to link the two up, I mean the train and the sub." He made a quick calculation. "I reckon at a steady forty to fifty miles an hour, these Germans should be approaching Josselin early tomorrow morning. So Captain, you'd have to send in your team tonight."

"Can do," Hurd replied hastily and for a few minutes the two officers discussed the details of the reconnaissance mission, while Mrs Smith listened, her face impassive, revealing nothing.

But when they had finished her conversation, she broke her silence to say, "It would useful to hear what these Japanese submariners are talking about among themselves, when they think they are not being overhead."

They looked at her startled and Hurd said, "I couldn't allow a woman to go on a mission like that. You're a civilian, not a member of His Majesty's forces. Besides, you'd have to be able to paddle a canoe for statters."

She gave him a little smile. "I was the United Universities champion in white water canoeing for two years running before the war. I would guess, in all modesty, that I've had more experience with canoes than you have, ever since I was a child in Japan."

Hurt actually blushed.

Fleming pursed his lips. "It would be useful. But you know you'd be taking an awful risk, Mrs Smith. If you were caught, your former fellow countrymen might take you for a spy and shoot you."

"I'm prepared to take that risk, Commander. It was a fate that my poor dear husband suffered. He was working with the S.O.E.* behind the Japanese lines in Burma when they caught him. "Fleming thought he caught the glint of tears in her dark eyes as she paused for a moment. "They shot him because he spoke their language. I owe it to my husband and all the rest of those brave young men who have died already, to help to bring this war to an end as soon as possible. It is my duty, too, to the country which has adopted me and made me one of its own. I am prepared to go."

A little helplessly Fleming looked at Hurd. Slowly the latter nodded his head. Mrs Smith could go. The dye was cast. Outside the guns started to thunder once more around Lorient. The Americans were attacking again.

* Wartime British intelligence and sabotage organization.

Chapter Two

Now the little train was chugging steadily through the high plain out of the Vosges. On both sides the fields were bare and everywhere there were still the scars of war, as if the French peasants had lost heart and had made no attempt to fill in the shell holes everywhere, and clear the rusting wrecks of the summer battles away. Indeed the whole landscape seemed sterile and dead, with only occasionally a house glimpsed where there was some kind of life.

Most of the Wotan troopers, bored by the lifelessness of scenery, slept, for although they knew their lives were forfeit if they were caught now, like all old soldiers they knew, too, it was wise to grab some sleep whenever they could.

Not so von Dodenburg and *Standartenführer* Zander. They pored over the big map of France, as the V-Mail Express headed steadily westwards. Both men knew little how railway signal systems operated. But as Zander said, "I'm hoping that the frog signals think because this is an *Ami* military train, it won't stick to the rules, their rules at least. The driver and his mate will have to do what we want because if they don't . . ." He made a clicking motion with his thumb and forefinger, as if firing a pistol.

Von Dodenburg laughed drily. "With Corporal Matz

– er – *attending* to them up front in the cab, I think you're right, Heinz," he said. "He's one person *I* wouldn't like to meet on a dark night."

Zander joined him and laughed, too. "I get your point!" Then he was serious. "Now we're on the final stage but one, of our long journey, I shall let you in on the great secret."

Von Dodenburg tensed. This was it, he told himself.

"Our destination is Lorient."

Von Dodenburg looked at Zander aghast. "But," he stuttered, "Lorient has been under siege by the *Amis* for weeks now. They're not going to let this train through with us, with a bow and have a good journey, gentlemen."

Zander laughed at the shocked look on von Dodenburg's harshly handsome face. "No, I don't think they would, Kuno. But we shall be dumping this train before we reach Lorient. Then we shall use another means of getting into the place and delivering what we have to deliver."

"And then?" von Dodenburg persisted. "What then? Are we going to sit out the rest of the war in a sort of self-run POW camp, which is what Lorient really is?"

"No, Kuno. You and the cadre of your regiment are far too valuable for *Reichsführer* Himmler to allow you to do that. The Führer has planned a great new offensive in the West for the winter. As far as I know, you and your regiment are going to lead one of the main thrusts into the *Ami* lines. No, as soon as we deliver – er – the goods, we are all to be brought out immediately and returned to the Reich."

At this stage von Dodenburg thought it wasn't wise to ask how. First they had to reach Lorient. But his mind raced electrically at the knowledge that the Führer was going to attack in the West once more, so soon after the terrible defeat in France. Was there still hope for the Reich after all, he asked himself.

A few seats away, *Bankdirektor* Grimm was quite sure that whatever Hitler attempted, the war was already lost for Germany. Now he, too, pored over the map of France wondering where it was best for him to take whatever loot he could carry, and begin his trek to a neutral country where he could begin a new life.

He had already decided he must head first for Spain. He had good contacts with important people in Madrid's *Banco de Espana*. He was sure that with the right amount of grease they could get him a passport and the means of leaving Spain for South America.

For a moment he indulged himself with a vision of a lazy life in some remote South American republic, perhaps on a beach by the warm ocean with a young Senorita, all flashing dark eyes, white teeth and splendid breasts, to attend to all his needs.

He licked his thin lips at the thought. Why not, he asked himself. He had worked all his life, day in, day out, to come home each night to Gertrud and her eternal complaint, "Oh, you men! That's all you beasts think about – woman on her back with her legs spread." And then afterwards, the perpetual moan, "Oh, aren't you finished with this beastly business *yet*?"

He dismissed the vision, delightful as it was, and concentrated on the task at hand. First he must get to Spain. He stared hard at the map through his pince-nez.

He sucked his teeth. Back in '42 he had conferred with officials of the *Credit Lyonnaise* about the confiscation of Jewish property and assets in Unoccupied France. He had offered them the Reichsbank's expertise in such matters. After all, the Reichsbank had been dealing with the damn Yids since '33 and had had a lot of experience in such matters. During the course of that week in France two years before, he had got on famously with the Comte de Dole, one of the *Credit*'s senior officials, who hated the Jews with a passion; and the Comte had a summer house at Rennes, which was on their present route.

Grimm looked up from the map, an idea slowly beginning to unfurl in his mean little mind. If anyone could help him to get to Spain – for a consideration – would the Comte de Dole. Pleased with himself, he started to think hard . . .

Guarding the American postal clerks, Schulze wasn't doing much thinking, but he was doing a lot of watching. In particular, he had his gaze fixed on the huge coloured woman whom he had seen naked in the bunk of the 'O/C Trains' that dawn. The latter, ashen-faced and baggy-eyed, was currently sulking, with his clerks, frightened for the most part by these strange Germans who had seized their train so surprisingly and had brought the war into their cushy little world. They kept glancing at the huge German armed with the big 45 Colt apprehensively, as if he might mow them down at any moment.

Schulze, for his part, had not the least interest in the clerks or their boss. His mind was on the very basic problem of how he might get the big woman into bed. Already he had shown his very basic French, mostly picked up in brothels during the Occupation, that he was in no way racially prejudiced. He had said, "*Tu . . . moi jig-jig.*" He had made his meaning clear with an obscene gesture. "*Tu noir . . . max nix.*" To which she had replied in quite good German, "Black . . . white . . . I wouldn't jig-jig with you if your dong was green."

The remark had not rebuffed him. He still felt that

if he could get the big coloured woman to himself in some quiet corner, preferably in bed, she'd deliver the goods. "It's my good looks and charm, Matzi," as he had explained to his running mate before the latter had gone on guard on the footplate. "I know how to treat a woman proper. I don't stick it to them with my boots on like some people I know," he had looked pointedly at Matz, "I take 'em off. When a lady says to me, do you love me or is that a revolver sticking out of yer pocket. I tells straightout I love 'em and *then* I pull out my revolver." He had chuckled coarsely at his own supposed humour. "Sergeant Schulze, the last of the frigging romantics," Matz had sneered in return before departing.

But how? That was the question going through Schulze's big head constantly at the moment. First he had thought of offering her money, but all he had was worthless German marks. He had plenty of cigarettes and most German women, he knew, would do 'it' for a packet of precious 'cancer sticks'. But he had already seen she didn't smoke, as he had remarked to Matz, while they had been discussing this 'very serious problem', to which Matz had said cheekily, "Ner, but I bet she smokes other things."

In the end he had concluded that, "she's got to take me for what I am, Matzi, Mrs Schulze's handsome son. There's no other way of getting up her drawers, I think."

Then Schulze had it. The next time she went to the little lavatory at the end of the compartment, he'd follow her and damn the consequences. It wasn't the most romantic of places to make love, but there was no other alternative. He *had* to have her. Every time he thought of that black massive rump heaving to and fro he had a diamond cutter. No, it'd have to be the thunder box or nothing. Carefully be began to watch the whore, waiting for the first sign that she was going to move . . .

The little American spotter plane dropped out of the sky startingly and almost caught Matz off guard. Moving very quickly for a man with one leg, Matz backed into the shadow cast by the coal tender, saying warningly in his best French, "No stupid moves." He raised his Colt threateningly. The driver gulped and bent his head over his controls.

Now the little light plane flew the length of the train at almost stalling speed. From his vantage point, Matz could see the white face of the observer next to the pilot, as he craned his neck to look downwards. The plane flew to the end of the train and then making a tight turn, came back once more, flying not much higher than the telegraph poles on both sides of the battered track.

For what seemed an eternity it seemed to hover just above the locomotive. Matz had a bright idea. Thrusting his pistol into his belt, he stepped out of the shadows smiled and waved his hand happily at the two men in the cockpit.

The trick worked. The two men waved back and then the plane departed, dragging its shadow across the fields until it disappeared into the distance. Matz gave a sigh of relief, though now he knew the same thing that von Dodenburg had realized when he had spotted the low-flying plane. "The only reason, Heinz," he said to Zander as the two of them watched the American plane, "that that spotter buzzed us is because the *Amis* have found something out."

Zander frowned. "But it's obvious, Kuno," he retorted, "that they don't know we have taken over this particular train. Otherwise they would have come with bombs and the like."

"Agreed," Von Dodenburg said with a worried look on his face. "But they certainly know something. Heinz," he stared hard at the one-eyed SS General, "we've got to be prepared to change our plans . . ."

Chapter Three

Almost noiselessly the two folboots glided down the estuary towards Lorient. This time Fleming was taking no chances that the two crews would run into trouble. An air raid had been, arranged. A squadron of RAF Lancaster bombers on their way to bomb Ludwigshafen in Germany would drop a couple of bombs of Lorient. By this means, Fleming hoped attention would be directed at the sky and not at the estuary. Now the two crews, Captain Hurd and Mrs Smith, and Corporal White and Marine Mendelsohn, waited for the first wail of the sirens indicating that Bomber Harris's boys were on their way.

Expertly Mrs Smith, sitting behind Hurd, propelled the folboot forward, hardly making a flurry with her paddle as she placed it in and out of the water. Hurd nodded his approval. Mrs Smith knew her business all right. Still he was worried. After all she was a civilian and a woman at that.

Now the submarine pens at Lorient, squat and broad, started to loom up once more. Somewhere there was the sound of hammering and the hiss of a blow torch. Obviously the Germans were working inside the pens. Hurd looked pensive and wondered if they were working on the Japanese submarine.

Minutes passed leadenly. There was a breeze blowing

and it kept blowing the freezing spray over the two of them, but still Mrs Smith continued her paddling, as if she hadn't noticed the cold. Hurd told himself there'd be a hard frost before dawn. He hoped that they would find out what they wanted and be on their way back before that happened. Once the folboots started to freeze over, they became damnably difficult to steer.

There it was! The first shrill wail of the air raid, signalling the start of a raid. All around the beleaguered port, the searchlights clicked on and started parting the clouds with their icy-white fingers. The RAF was on its way.

Hurd increased the tempo. It didn't matter about sound now. The sirens and soon the bombers would drown any sound they might make. Behind him Mrs Smith kept up effortlessly. She was not even breathing hard. He shook his head in admiration. To their rear the other two marines started paddling more quickly, too, to keep up.

The bombers hit Lorient five minutes later. They could hear the shriek of the bombs quite clearly, as the four-engined planes passed overhead, ignoring the scarlet stabs of flame as the flak opened up at them, the pilots knowing that this was a diversion and it didn't matter whether they hit their target or not.

Hurd told himself that it was hard on the long-suffering French civilians who were trapped in the besieged port. But at the same time he reasoned that most of them were actively working with the Germans so perhaps they deserved what was coming to them.

They came to the same jetty where they had tied up the folboat the last time. Hurd signalled to Mrs Smith to stop paddling and they glided noiselessly to the spot where he would anchor their little craft. Corporal White did the same.

To their front, the bombs were thudding into the thick concrete hide of the submarine pens, exploding in dramatic flashes of yellow and white flame as the flak guns thundered, sending their shells speeding into the night sky. Hurd knew that the bombs would have no effect. The RAF and the US 8th Air Force in Britain had been trying to knock out Lorient's sub pens for years. To no avail. Still the bombs did provide the cover they needed.

He took Mrs Smith's hand as they clambered to the base of the jetty. "Do you need any help getting up there?" he asked and added with an attempt at humour, "Don't tell me you're a mountain climber as well as a skilled canoeist?"

"No," she answered in a whisper. "But I have done a lot of hill walking with my late husband."

He gave a mock groan. "All right," he said, "get on with it, but make as little noise as possible. I think the Brylcreem boys," he meant the RAF bombers, "are about finished with their little diversion."

Quickly Mrs Smith scuttled up the sheer wall onto the quay and was followed immediately by the other three men of the SBS. For a moment or two they crouched there, as over Lorient the sirens started to sound the 'all clear' and the drone of the bombers, still pursued by the flak, began to die away.

Hurd blinked his eyes to accustom them to the darkness after the searchlights were extinguished one by one. He peered around. The quay was deserted. Not even a sentry. "All right," he whispered, "we'll try the sub pen first. Let's see what we can make out there. And be careful. The sub pen is always occupied with workmen and sentries. OK, let's go, chaps."

Sticking close to the shadows of the 18th-century

merchants' houses which lined the quay, the four of them stole forward. Lorient, it seemed, had gone back to sleep after the short raid, but there was a persistent hollow clang of hammering coming from the pens and Hurd told himself that the Germans were working at something important. Why else should they be hammering at this time of the night?

Now the submarine pen, from which the noise came, was right in front of them. Hurd told the others to wait, while he went forward, crouching low, hardly daring to breathe. He peered in at the long stretch of water covered by the tremendously thick concrete roof. There lay the Japanese submarine, bigger than any submarine he had ever seen before, the rising sun flag of Imperial Japan drooping at its stern.

German workers, civilian and military, were everywhere and Hurd told himself that he didn't need a crystal ball to know that they were preparing the sub for a long voyage. Indeed he could see the usual stores piled up on the side of the pen, which submarines needed to keep them running for several weeks at sea: tinned goods, salamis, dried hams, a hundred and one things. He nodded his head. The Jap sub was definitely going to run out to sea soon.

Silently he backed off to where the others were waiting. Hurriedly he told them what he had seen and then added, "Let's go to the place where we took the prisoner last time. Do you remember exactly how to get there, Chalky?"

White grinned in the darkness. "How could I forget, sir, with that bint with her—" He stopped short, embarrassed, as he realized that Mrs Smith was listening, too. "I'll get you there, sir," he added hurriedly.

They stole away, retracing their way down the cobbled streets of the old port, to where the brothel was situated.

Again the streets were deserted, for it was long after curfew. Now, Hurd knew, that the only people they might encounter in Lorient would be enemy troops. He felt inside his pocket for the reassurance of the butt of his pistol, already fitted with a silencer.

"To the right," White directed.

Hurd turned in the direction indicated. He could already hear the clash of cymbals and the hectic beat of a drum. They were dancing again in the brothel. He wondered if there would be Japs there again and whether they could find out more by listening to them. At all events, they already knew the Jap submarine was preparing for departure. That would interest Commander Fleming for certain.

The patrol caught them completely off guard. Instead of the stamp of nailed jackboots which would have alerted them to the approach of the enemy, this was the muffled shuffle of rubber-soled shoes on the cobbles. Suddenly, frighteningly, there they were helmeted Japanese soldiers, with at their head a bespectacled officer trailing a long sabre behind him.

"Halt!" the officer cried in German, "*Wer da?*"

Hurd pulled out his pistol.

The officer was quicker. He pulled out the curved sword and sliced it through the air. Hurd yelped with pain. The silenced pistol clattered to the cobbles, as he staggered back, the blood jetting in a scarlet arc from his nearly severed right arm.

White tried to unsling his sten gun. To no avail! One of the patrol thrust with his bayonet. He screamed in agony, face contorted, as the sharp point of the bayonet penetrated his guts. "Cor ferk a duck," he began, as the Japanese sailor withdrew the blood-stained bayonet with an obscene slithering sound. Then he collapsed on his knees on the cobbles, the blood surging through his fingers as he tried to hold his guts in. Next moment he slapped to the *pavé*, his intestines slithering out of the wound like a grey-pink steaming snake.

The sailor yelled in triumph. He raised the bayonetted rifle above his head as if he were about to plunge it into the back of the dying corporal, who was threshing his legs and moaning in his death throes.

Mrs Smith's hands flew to her mouth in horror. But she managed to keep her nerve. With all the authority she could muster, she shouted "*Eya!*"*

The sailor paused in mid-stride. He swung his head round to see what the officer's reaction was.

The latter stared dumbfounded at Mrs Smith.

"*Kami sama*," the officer exclaimed in amazement, adding in broken German. "Do Nippom?"

She nodded wildly, as corporal Chalky White died at their feet. "*Hi . . . hi . . .*"

The little officer with the sabre recovered quickly. "*Keimusho*," he barked. "Prison . . . prison. *Hayai . . .*"†

Inwardly Mrs Smith groaned. She knew now what she could expect.

---

* No in Japanese. *Transl.*
† Quick. *Transl.*

Chapter Four

It had started to snow again, bitter relentless flakes which came down with a fury, as if some God on high was determined to blot out the war torn landscape below. But even the hiss of the storm couldn't drown out the noise of the aircraft's engine, as the little light plane started to circle the train below.

Von Dodenburg looked at Zander as they both cocked their heads to one side so that they could hear more clearly. The SS General looked worried, and von Dodenburg knew why. It couldn't just be a coincidence that they were being checked out yet again from the air. Had the Americans already learned that the 'V-Mail Express' was on its usual route back to the port of Cherbourg, but had now changed to another line which would take due south-west? Von Dodenburg put his anxious thoughts into words, "What do you think, Heinz?"

"The same as you, Kuno, I suspect. The *Amis* are on to us."

Now they could see the plane, as it emerged from the snowstorm. It was flying very low and very slow, almost at tree-top height, with the face of the pilot and his observer clearly visible, as they stared down at the little train.

"Do you think they've got radio contact with their field?" Zander asked.

"I should think so. But if you're thinking what I am, Heinz," vom Dodenburg added with a sudden smile, "*accidents*," he emphasized, "do happen in weather like this, don't they?"

Now it was Zander's turn to smile. "Exactly. And I think it's time for that American gentleman up there to have an accident."

A few seats away, Grimm watched the plane too, and came to the same conclusion as the two SS officers. This time it wasn't just chance that the Americans in their plane were watching them. Somehow they had aroused suspicion. He licked his suddenly dry lips. What would those SS swine do now, he asked himself. If they did what he thought they might well do, it might be just as well to start carrying out his own personal plan.

Grimm looked to left and right. But everybody in the coach was concentrating on the plane above, as it came round once more and started to fly the length of the train. He fumbled in his waistcoat for the key and then he rose and went out.

Schulze, in the next compartment, gave Grimm a passing glance as he went to the middle coach, in which the gear they had brought with them from Alsace was stored. Then he concentrated his attention again on the coloured woman. He had personally seen to it that she had more to drink than the other prisoners.

Now to his glee she was beginning to wriggle on her seat as if she were feeling a strong urge to use the little lavatory at the end of the corridor. He made his move. With apparent casualness he opened the door of the compartment and went out to post himself where she would have to pass if she went to the lavatory, licking his lips in anticipation of the pleasures to come . . .

* * *

Hastily von Dodenburg balanced the light machine gun on the open window frame. The plane was coming in for another run. He knew as he lined up in his sights that he'd get only one chance. If he started firing and missed, the American plane would be off to report that it had been fired upon; then, as the Wotan's stubble hoppers always phrased it, 'the clock wouldn't certainly be in the pisspot.' He clenched his face grimly. He simply couldn't afford to miss.

"All right, Kuno," Heinz snapped, feeding the long belt of ammunition into the machine gun, "knock the *Ami* bastard out of the sky!"

Von Dodenburg nodded but said nothing. He was concentrating all his attention on the light spotter plane as it came lower and lower. Automatomatically he tucked the butt of the gun more firmly into his right shoulder and closed one eye. He peered along the long air-cooled barrel. The little plane filled the whole of his foresight now. He controlled his breathing. Slowly, carefully, he began to take first pressure, his forefinger curled around the trigger of the machine gun.

Standartenführer Zander watched him tensely. He, too, knew what was at stake. If von Dodenburg didn't knock the enemy plane out of the sky with his first burst, they were sunk. Within the hour, the *Amis* would be flinging everything, including the kitchen stove, at them.

Schulze gave a chuckle of delight. The big coloured woman had just opened the door of the compartment, holding her hand pressed between her legs like small children do when they need to go to the lavatory urgently.

With a bow, he opened the door of the little toilet, crying in his best French, "*Pour votre plaisir, m'selle.*"

She made an obscene gesture with her middle finger and brushed by him so close that he could feel those magnificent haunches press momentarily against his loin. He gasped with pleasure, as she shut the door in his face, crying, in German, "No looking, arse-with-ears."

Again he bowed and said, "You have my word of honour, m'selle, as a gentleman of the old school."

There was the sound of liquid gushing urgently. Schulze licked his lips once again, visualizing already that delightful spot from where that liquid stemmed. I could eat it with a knife and fork, he thought to himself, without salt and pepper at that.

The lavatory flushed and she came out, hurriedly adjusting her skirt though he did manage to catch a glimpse of a great black thigh above the top of her stockings. "That's a fine sight for a man. Warms the cockles of your heart on the cold day like this."

"Well, that's all that's going to be warmed," she snapped and started to brush by him. Schulze let his hands drop on her well-rounded rump as she did so, and pressed his fingers onto her flesh.

"Get off my meat," she cried. "If yer want it, yer've got to pay for it." And with that and a flighty toss of her head she was gone, leaving Schulze with a burning sensation in his groin, but nothing else.

Von Dodenburg pressed the trigger in the same instant that Matz up on the cab, watching the fireman and train driver, ordered the latter to stop the engine. *Wham . . . wham . . . wham.* The bullets zipped towards the surprised plane. The perspex of the cockpit shattered. A line of gleaming bullet holes ran the length of the fuselage. The engine spluttered, sprang into life once more and spluttered again.

"Holy strawsack!" Zander yelled excitedly. "You've got him, Kuno!"

Madly the pilot tried to control the plane. To no avail. The engine went dead for good. Von Dodenburg let the plane have another burst. Like a stone the little aircraft fell out the sky. It slammed into the field on the left of the track, bounced high in the air momentarily and then crashed down again. The undercarriage gave way. A wheel trundled off. An instant later the engine burst into flames. No one got out.

Up on the cab, Matz shoved the pistol into the ribs of the driver menacingly, not seeing the figure stealing from the train into the woods to the right. "*Los*," he commanded.

The driver jerked down his lever hurriedly. The wheels shuddered and clattered on the frozen railtracks. The driver cursed and released some sand so that they could get a grip. Steam poured from the boiler as the steel pistons worked to and fro and the little train started to move once more.

Schulz spotted the burning plane and told himself he had missed all the action; he had been too concerned with the big French woman. But it hadn't worked. The woman was right. He needed something to pay her for the pleasure of having her open 'them pearly gates', as he would have phrased it. But he had nothing, save worthless German marks and some looted francs taken off the prisoners which weren't much better.

Suddenly his eye caught something glittering on the floor of the corridor. He frowned, wondering what it was. After a moment's hesitation, he bent and picked it up. In the increased light it glittered ever more. He frowned even more. Could it be some kind of jewel? he asked himself. But where would something like that come from, on a shitty rundown American train?

He thought of that splendid rump and that beautiful milk factory the French whore had in her blouse. By God, he could get his head between those tits and not see or hear a thing for a month or two. Now if this were really a diamond. He licked his lips, his mind already full of the delights she could offer him. But who would know whether it was a diamond or just a piece of glass?

The officers of course. They would know about such things. Officers always knew about such matters. They taught them that sort of thing at their cadet schools, where they learned how to hold a champagne glass level with the third button of their tunic and how to address a general's wife in the third person plural – all that sort of classy stuff.

His mind made up, hampered a little by a half erection already, he made his way back to where Zander and von Dodenburg were relaxing a little, now that the American spotter plane had been dealt with. He snapped to attention and bellowed, as if he were back on the parade ground in Berlin before the war. "*Oberscharführer Schulze meldet sich zur Stelle and mochte—*"

"Cut out the crap, Schulze," von Dodenburg interrupted him brutally. "What are you up to now?"

"Like a piece of advice, sir," Schulze said dutifully.

Von Dodenburg laughed hollowly. "Since when did you take advice, Schulze? But go on – fire away."

"This, sir." Schulze opened a paw like a small steam hammer and revealed the gem lying there in his palm. "Do you think that's the real thing?" he asked hopefully, his mind already full of the French whore, with her big legs draped over his naked shoulders.

Before von Dodenburg could answer, Zander asked sharply, "Where did you get it?"

"Found it down the corridor, sir," Schulze answered.

Von Dodenburg looked from Schulze to Zander a little helplessly, as if asking himself what was going on.

"Next to the coach where – the – er cargo is, Sergeant?"

"Yes sir."

Zander flashed a look to where Grimm had been sitting until the American spotter plane had appeared on the scene. The seat was empty. "Holy shit!" he exclaimed angrily. "Grimm's gone and done a bunk . . ."

Chapter Five

The squat little Japanese officer with the horn-rimmed glasses shouted something at Mrs Smith in Japanese.

She was pale and obviously afraid, but she kept her nerve. She said as firmly as she could, "*Nihon go ga wakerimasen.** Please speak English."

The little Japanese officer flushed with rage. He drew back his hand and then slapped her savagely on both cheeks.

Hurd, his arm roughly attended to, tried to get up from the floor of the barracks room in which they were holding him. But the elderly Gestapo man in his creaking green leather coat hit him and he fell down again, moaning with the pain of his wound.

"All right," the Japanese officer, said. "We speak English, bitch." His dark eyes bored into the woman prisoner. "You tell me what you do here?"

"We were trying to find out where your submarine was going," Mrs Smith said in a low voice, avoiding looking at her interrogator.

"You lie . . . you spy," the Japanese officer cried in fury. He slapped her again.

Hurd said, "Stop that, you swine!"

The Gestapo man shook his head in warning. He'd

---

* "I don't speak Japanese." *Transl.*

seen this kind of interrogation often enough. The little yellow ape, he told himself, was working himself up to a fury, an artificial rage, which would frighten the prisoner and then allow him vent that rage in physical form if the prisoner didn't confess. It was an old trick.

For his part, he was going to keep his nose clean. The war would be over soon and undoubtedly he'd be a prisoner sooner or later, and he didn't want any charges of torture brought against him. He wanted to go home to mother pretty damn quick. Still he watched with interest, as the Jap started to try to break the woman down.

"Well?" he demanded. "You speak?"

She shook her head boldly. "I have told all I know."

The Japanese officer barked something at her in Japanese.

Again she shook her head, now not trusting herself to speak.

The Japanese officer started to tremble with rage, his overlong sword rattling as he did so. He bellowed to the two guards and when one of them wasn't quick enough for him, he slapped him across the face. The young Japanese sailor bowed several times, the fingermarks made by the slap clearly visible on his yellow face.

Now the two of them seized Mrs Smith. She struggled. In vain.

They were too strong for her. While one held her, the other ripped down the front of her blouse. Her breasts fell out and she tried to cover them shamefacedly. But the sailor holding her didn't give her a chance. He held her tight.

The officer barked an order and the old Gestapo man waited expectantly. He guessed what was coming. It was something that would never be tolerated in the Gestapo. The rating who had been slapped tugged at her skirt. It came away. Next moment he ripped down her knickers, leaving her looking naked and absurd at the same time.

"You swine." Hurd gasped, again struggling to rise to his feet as the tears started to stream silently down Mrs Smith's ashen face. "You'll pay for this, if it's the last thing I do on this earth."

At the other side of the room Marine Mendelsohn forgot his own fears. He had recognized the old man in the green leather coat immediately as a Gestapo man and as German-Jewish refugee, who had fled to England with his parents back in 1938, he had no wish to draw attention to himself. All the same he knew he had to try to something. He couldn't allow them to humiliate this poor brave woman who had volunteered to go with them on this dangerous mission. *But what*?

Slowly, deliberately, the little Japanese officer stared up and down Mrs Smith's naked middle-aged body. His yellow face contorted with contempt as he glanced at her poor drooping breasts and then the sparsely-haired vulva.

The Gestapo man chewed the butt of his half smoked cheap cigar to one side of his mouth and then to the other, wondering what the little yellow ape would do next. He forgot about the other prisoners, concentrating on the Japanese officer and the naked woman.

The officer took his time. He was breaking the woman down mentally first. Then he would commence the physical side of the torture. Almost gently he reached out his right hand and touched her breast.

The woman flinched and tried to pull back, but the ratings held her tightly. Smiling and showing a mouthful of gold teeth, the officer tweaked her nipple, while on the floor the wounded Hurd raged in impotent fury. For his part, Mendelsohn watched the fat Gestapo thug, who was staring at the torture victim with undisguised lust now. Was the Japanese going to rape the poor woman or something? Did the Gestapo man know that?

The interrogator dropped his hand and caressed the woman's wrinkled stomach. He ran his fingers lightly down the appendix scar there.

"You speak now," he demanded in English, fingers poised at the top of Mrs Smith's thinning pubic hair. "Yes?"

She pressed her lips together till they were white, as if she dare not open her mouth in case she revealed all.

The officer turned to the bigger of the two ratings and barked an order.

The sailor hesitated.

Without blinking an eye, the officer slapped him left and right across the face. The rating's face burned but he submitted to the treatment. He began to fumble with his flies.

The Gestapo man licked his fat sensuous lips. The Nip was going to put on a show. This was going to be interesting. On the floor Hurd watched in horror as the sailor brought out his penis and started manipulating it, while the officer waited impatiently.

The sailor was young and apparently very virile. He was erect within seconds.

The officer yelled another order. The second rating held on to a terrified Mrs Smith more tightly, as she whimpered, "Please . . . please no!"

Awkwardly, with his penis erect, the young sailor approached Mrs Smith. "*Sumimusen*," he whispered as he closed with the woman. "Sorry." He put his hands around her buttocks and pulled her towards him in the same moment that Mendelsohn acted. He sprang

149

forward. The Gestapo officer was caught completely off guard. Mendelsohn, tough and supremely fit like all the SBS marines, grabbed him and held him like a shield in front of him, crying in German, "*Keine Bewegung oder Sie sind tot!*"

The Japanese officer let out a great roar of rage. He sprang forward, tugging at his absurdly long sword, face red with anger. Mendelsohn beat him to it. He tugged Hurd's silenced pistol from the Gestapo man's pocket aimed and fired in one and the same moment.

The officer stopped in mid-stride. His hand dropped from the hilt of his sword and he stared momentarily at the great red hole in stomach, as if he couldn't comprehend how it had got there. Then he gave a soft moan and crumpled to the floor unconscious.

Mendelsohn propelled the Gestapo man towards the two dumbfounded Japanese ratings, who just stood there, the one with his now flaccid penis in his hand, wondering what to do. "Take off your pistol belt," he ordered the Gestapo man, "*slowly*." All the time he kept the silenced pistol levelled at the two Japanese.

With fingers that trembled violently, the policeman did as he was ordered.

"Drop it to the floor – carefully," Mendelsohn commanded.

The fat cop did so and with the back of his heel Mendelsohn shoved the belt and pistol in Hurd's direction. The wounded officer grabbed it eagerly with his good hand. He pulled out the pistol, clicked off the safety and cried, "Have 'em covered, Mendelsohn."

"Good sir," Mendelsohn said, without taking his gaze off the two sailors for one instant. "Now Mrs Smith, tell them to let you go and see what you can do about your dress."

"Thank you ... oh, thank you," Mrs Smith said fervently, the tears of joy and relief streaming down her poor tortured face. She said something in Japanese. The one rating let go of his hold. Immediately Mrs Smith pulled herself together and tried to cover herself the best she could.

Mendelsohn waited till she had hidden her breasts and pulled up her knickers, though he knew everything depended upon getting out of the Gestapo HQ as quickly as possible. Someone else might turn up and that would be that. Time was of the essence. "What now, sir?" he called over to Hurd on the floor, without taking his eyes off their prisoners for one moment.

"Get those two Japs to get me to my feet," Hurd said weakly. "I'll make it once I'm up. We'll take their car. Hurry."

Mrs Smith forgot her appearance. She said something in Japanese to the two ratings. Willingly enough they hurried forward to pick up the wounded officer. Hurd groaned but he managed it. "Now," he said, trying to put some resolve into his voice, though the pain was very severe. "We'll never get back to the boats. We've got to try to bluff our way through the German lines to the Yanks. It's a tall order, but it's the only way. You speak German Mendelsohn, you'll have to do it."

"I'll do my best, sir," Mendelsohn replied loyally.

Then they were out of the villa, which served as Gestapo HQ in Lorient, heading for the car and the unknown before them.

Chapter Six

"Did I ever tell you my old dad used to take to his false teeth and play *Deutschland über alles* on them with a spoon? Though he was a Communist, he was very patriotic," Schulze added, well pleased with himself.

He had shown the coloured woman the diamond and she had agreed to pleasure him at the first possible opportunity for it. "I show you good time, soldier boy," she had promised and had run her tongue slowly around her thick red lips. "You like a lot."

"I'd like a lot at this very moment," Schulze had answered, grabbing for her massive bosom.

But she had warded him off, saying, "Now, naughty boy. You wait." Now Schulze was waiting. Impatiently.

"So what's this about your old man?" Matz asked without interest. "Did he ever marry yer mother by the way?"

Schulze ignored the insult. Instead he said, "I was just thinking about him that's all. Yer know he lived to be eighty and he only snuffed it cos he tried to pleasure an 18-year-old twice in the same night. His poor old pump couldn't take it. Dead on the job," Schulze sighed fondly.

"What a way to go," Matz agreed. "That's how I'd like to croak – in the arms of a *bad* woman."

"The way things are going, we'll probably end up

with a bullet in our balls. That's why yer average stubble hopper's got to grab a little bit o' pleasure when he can."

Matz looked at him darkly. "Yer, you're gonna have a bit with that whore now you've got the diamond. But what about me, yer old comrade?"

"Find yer own frigging diamond," Schulze said unfeelingly.

"But with a rock like that, there should be enough for the two of us," Matz protested.

Schulze looked at him, as if he were mad. "What kind of wet fart are you? Don't yer realize with what I've got on board, one diamond won't be enough to pay the pavement pounder for her services." He looked down the corridor in anticipation. But the coloured woman was no where in sight. Schulze sighed and stared moodily out of the window.

In the middle coach which held the secret cargo, *Standartenführer* Zander did the same, watching the empty countryside hurry by, as they rolled ever westwards. He knew he would have to make a decision so on, but which? The choice was difficult, damnably difficult.

Von Dodenburg took his eyes off the jewel boxes which Grimm had plundered before he sneaked off the train with his loot, heading for some destination known only to himself. He put Zander's thoughts into words for him, then he knew the time had come to make that overwhelming decision. "Heinz, if Grimm is picked up, which he might well be, the mission is compromised. They'll do all they can to stop this train before we ever reach Lorient."

Zander nodded dourly.

"If he isn't picked up and we do manage to reach Lorient, how will we ever get out again? There we'd be nearly four hundred kilometres from the nearest German positions around Colmar in Alsace."

Again Zander nodded sombrely, but this time he broke his silence. "Yes, Kuno, I've been thinking on those terms ever since Grimm vanished. If the *Amis* or the Frogs do pick him up, he'll squeal all right. But that's not all. I think he knows the additional cargo we are carrying is of world-shaking importance. To save his own skin, Grimm will tell the enemy as much as he knows about. He'll tell them about the atomic bomb plans which we are delivering to the Japs."

"So that's the name of that terrible weapon you told me about, Heinz."

"Yes," Zander said. "But now with Grimm gone I'm having my doubts about it." He looked worried. "But if I don't deliver, I, you, perhaps all your Wotan troopers, too, will face the Führer's wrath. It could mean the execution of all of us."

Von Dodenburg thought for a moment before he asked, "How exactly, when we abandoned the train, were we supposed to get into Lorient? It would be pretty difficult to pass through the American lines I would have thought."

"No, the plan is for us not to attempt to pass through the *Ami* lines," Zander replied. "There is a little independent British commando unit – at least we think they are some sort of commando unit – at a small fishing port just north of Lorient. A place called Port Aven. Air reconnaissance has shown they've got a variety of small boats and canoes, plus a small tramp steamer, which is obviously used to bring men and supplies from England and the like.

"It was Himmler's intention to seize that boat with your men – that is why we needed the whole of what is left of Wotan for the job – and force the crew to sail her to Lorient. There the authorities would be warned and they would trawl a way free of mines for us up the estuary."

Von Dodenburg whistled softly, quite impressed. "Hat's off to the planners!" he exclaimed. "That certainly is something that the enemy wouldn't expect."

"That is what we thought. Seize the boat at night and we'd be in Lorient before first light on the following morning. The darkness would give us the cover we need from their air."

"Exactly," von Dodenburg agreed enthusiastically. Then the animation vanished from his handsome young face as he remembered the situation they found themselves in. Now he phrased the overwhelming question that had just flashed through his mind carefully, very carefully. "Heinz," he said, "but if we capture that boat, do we *have* to sail it to Lorient?"

"How do you mean, Kuno?"

"Couldn't we use it for our own purposes – to get Wotan back to the nearest German lines, say in Holland?" He warned to the theme. "It's an English ship, with English markings and the like. If we destroy these commandos' communications, we could be well on our way before the enemy discovered what had happened."

"But Kuno," Zander protested, "how do I explain that we didn't deliver those top secret papers?"

"You don't have to explain it, Heinz," von Dodenburg replied.

"How do you mean?" the other man demanded sharply.

"The V-Mail Express will be destroyed – by enemy action, together with the great secret."

"But how do we know that, Kuno?" Zander demanded, puzzled.

Von Dodenburg chuckled softly. "Because *we* do the destroying. Therefore, there will be no need for us to continue our mission. Then it will be a question of *sauve que veut*. Who can hold that against us – brave soldiers of the elite SS Wotan returning to the Fatherland to continue the great struggle?"

Zander took in the suggestion slowly. He scratched the back of his shaven head and sucked in his cheeks like a man who was doing a great deal of rapid thinking. "But Kuno," he said slowly, "we would be destroying a great secret, one that might win the peace for Germany, you know."

"I've considered that, Heinz," von Dodenburg answered smartly. "But if our scientists couldn't make this – er – atomic bomb of yours, what hope have the Japs? And time is running our for Germany – fast. The enemy is already at our borders to east and west. It won't be long before they attack across those borders."

"The Führer's great offensive—" Zander began to say but von Dodenburg cut him short with an angry wave of his hand. "We scraping the bottom of the barrel for men and machines, Heinz, and you know it. Where will the Führer find the dozens of new divisions he would need to defeat the Anglo-Americans? Look at the state of Wotan. A couple of hundred men left out of nearly three thousand last June. No," he snorted angrily, "we've got to save our own skins and those of my young troopers. That's what's important now, Heinz. It's five minutes to midnight as you well know." He paused, chest heaving a little with so much rapid talking and waited for Zander's reaction.

Zander nodded. "I understand, Kuno. Our first loyalty is to ourselves and those under our command. God knows what will happen to us as senior SS officers, if the Allies win. They'll probably castrate us first so we can't breed again." He favoured von Dodenburg with that same tough, reckless grin that von Dodenburg remembered from the old days in Russia when it was victory after victory. For a moment he looked around at the young troopers lying sprawled in their seats, sleeping or smoking. "But that's Germany's future, isn't it, those young troopers of yours."

"Yes it is, Heinz. Up to now they have learned how to die for Germany. Now the time has come for them to learn how to *live* for the country. What do you say, Heinz. Is it a go?"

Zander stuck out his one hand. "It's a go, Kuno," he said, voice filled with sudden determination. "We'll get what's left of Wotan back – come what may. Now let's look at it like this, Kuno, old house . . ."

Ten metres away, the coloured woman looked over her big shoulder and winked hugely. Then she turned and placed her brown hands under her massive bosom, and gave it a great heave as if she were getting it into place for what was to come. Schulze swallowed hard and choked, "Did you see that, Matzi? I'm on. She wants me to slip her a link." He rose from his wooden seat hastily and said, "I'm off. Wish me luck."

Matz looked up at him scornfully. "I hope you've got yer serial number stamped on the soles of yer boots in case I've got to identify you."

"Cheeky shit!" Schulze said without animosity. "She ain't *that* big."

Then he was off, already fumbling with his flies,

chanting, "Things are looking up . . . things are looking up all along the line."

Outside, the sky started to turn a threatening, leaden grey. It looked as if more snow was on the way.

Chapter Seven

"The Germans don't have a continuous line around Lorient," Hurd explained weakly from the back of the big Gestapo car, as they left the blacked-out industrial suburbs of Lorient and headed for the front. "They don't have enough troops for that. Instead they have a series of strongpoints linked to each other and with mutually supporting artillery. Do you follow me?"

Mandelsohn, now wearing the Gestapo officer's green leather coat and sitting next to their prisoner who was now driving, turned and asked, "Does that mean we can slip in between a couple of these strong points, sir?"

Hurt shook his head. "I doubt it. They'll probably have the unguarded spots covered by mines and the like. No, the only way is to talk our way through a strong point."

Mrs Smith, who had recovered her usual calmness, gently placed another towel over Hurd's wounded arm and said, "Have you any plan, Captain?"

"I thought, we could use me," Hurd answered somewhat mysteriously.

"*You?*"

"Yes. You are all in their uniform or in Japanese," he indicated the two totally confused young Japanese sailors sitting on the rumble seat opposite, "but I'm in British uniform. Let us say I'm a wounded British officer who needs urgent medical treatment he can't get in Lorient. So the German authorities are exchanging me for some high ranking German prisoner."

In the front seat, Mandelsohn said, "That's sounds a smashing idea." But almost immediately his enthusiasm waned. "But what about the Japs, sir and Mrs Smith? What will the Jerries make of they?"

"Hm, that *is* a bit of a stinker," Hurn agreed.

"Could I make a suggestion?" Mrs Smith asked in that quiet manner of hers.

"Yes please," Hurd said.

"I'm sure everybody in the garrison here knows that there is a Japanese submarine in Lorient now. After all, it is the only one in the port. We are from the submarine then, going on along to see what the brave German comrades are doing. But," she lowered her voice, "we're also out to see the lay of the land for the time when the sub makes its breakout."

Hurt considered for a moment and up in the front seat, Mandelsohn said, "Dr Goebbels, their Minister of Propaganda, always maintained, sir, if you are going to tell a lie, tell a big one. The Jerries might just buy it."

"All right, we'll have a go at it. And remember if anything goes wrong, surprise is the key. Make the square head there put his foot down hard and we'll fight it out if necessary."

Now they could see they were beginning to approach the German main line of defence. To their front flares were constantly zipping into the sky and now and again tracer cut the darkness lethally. Mandelsohn tensed, pistol on his lap. Now a lot was going to depend upon him, as the escapers' German speaker. Now he was dressed in Gestapo officer's greatcoat, he would have to sound arrogant and overbearing as the

Gestapo always were, knowing that even senior officers were afraid of what the secret police could do to them if they wished.

The Gestapo man at the wheel turned into a side road. The big car started to bump up and down on the rough cobbles of the *pavé*, lurching heavily every now and again when the front wheels hit a badly patched shell hole. On both sides there were wrecked, abondoned cottages and the occasional farm. As always, Mendelsohn told himself, the closer you get to the front, the lonelier the countryside seems.

They rode for another five or ten minutes. Now they were becoming aware that there were men on both sides of the road. Although the blackout was nearly perfect they did catch the odd quick chink of light as someone perhaps opened the door of a bunker and once they spotted a battery of howitzers covered with camouflage netting. "It won't be long now," Hurd whispered. "Stand by to do your best, Mendelsohn."

"Yessir." By way of a warning, Mendelsohn thrust the muzzle of his pistol into the driver's ribs hard. "Watch your step, copper," he snarled. "One wrong move and you're a dead man."

The Gestapo man started but he reacted quietly. "Don't worry, Mister Tommy, I'm not going to risk my life. Indeed in a way I'm grateful to you."

"*Grateful*," Mendelsohn echoed in surprise.

"Yes. If I'd sat it out in Lorient till the end, more than likely I would have been given to the frogs. And that wouldn't have been very nice. Ner, I don't mind ending up the war in a nice cushy English POW camp."

Mendelsohn shook his head in mock disbelief. "Well, I'll be damned!" he exclaimed.

They rolled on.

Now to their immediate front, in the middle of the little country road, they could see a shaded red light. By straining his eyes, Mendelsohn could just make out what the Germans called a '*Spanischer Reiter*', a wood and barbed wire barricade which could be moved easily by one man, but which at the same time effectively blocked the road. "Road barricade," he called to the others. "We're there." He poked the driver in the ribs once more. "Slow down. Act normal."

The Gestapo man did as he was ordered, peering to his front, trying to make out the details of the barricade and who was manning it.

"*Halt . . . Wer da?*" a stern voice commanded from out of the darkness.

The Gestapo man braked, but kept the car in gear and the motor running just in case. "*Geheime Staatspolizei*," the driver snapped. 'Secret State Police'. It was a name which usually impressed the average German.

The sentry flashed a torch into the car, apparently unimpressed, turning the beam from face to face slowly, while they blinked and tried to shield their eyes. He took in Mendelsohn in his green leather coat, then he flashed the beam on the passengers in the back. He gasped. "Hey, what's this? A wounded Tommy officer, a Jap woman and two Jap sailors. What in three devils' name is going on?"

Glibly Mendelsohn told him their cover story, while the sentry, just a dim outline to them, kept the beam of his torch levelled on them.

"Seems a rum'un to me," he commented when Mendelsohn was finished. "Exchanges . . . Japs spying. I don't know." The beam wavered a moment.

"You are not paid to think," Mendelsohn snapped, playing the worse kind of arrogant German officer. "And slap a 'sir' on it when you speak to me. Now here's my dog licence," he meant the dull metal badge of the Gestapo, "to show you we're genuine. See. Now get that damned barricade moved, toot sweet."

"All right, sir," the sentry grumbled. "I suppose it's all right."

"Of course it is, man," Mendelsohn barked, his heart beating like a trip hammer. "Move it and where are the closest *Ami* positions?"

"Just over there on the reverse slope of these low hills, sir," the sentry replied and started to move the wooden barrier with his one hand, holding the torch still in his other.

Mendelsohn swallowed hard. They were pulling it off. Next to him the Gestapo man was gunning his engine, prior to driving away. He didn't want it to stall at this juncture. Obviously he was nervous, too.

Now the way was almost free. Suddenly there came the sound of a telephone ringing in the little wooden shack next to the barrier. A voice said something. Mendelsohn heard someone say incredulously, "*Was sagen Sie?* – what do you say? "The phone was slammed down. A man ran out. "Stop that—"

The driver didn't wait to hear the rest. He let out the clutch and drove forward. Obviously someone had found the dead Jap and had alerted the post to look out for a stolen Mercedes. The right fender slammed into the side of the barricade. It lurched wildly. The Gestapo man used all his strength to keep the vehicle on the road. Shots rang out. Scarlet flame stabbed the darkness. Flares hissed into the night sky.

"Christ Almighty," Mendelsohn cursed, "the whole bleeding front's coming to life." He could hear the slugs slamming into the side of the car.

Now careening wildly from side to side on the narrow little country road, the Gestapo man drove all out. He knew his life would be forfeit, too, if they were taken now. A machine gun chattered into frenetic life to their left. The windscreen shattered into glittering a spider's web. Hastily, using the butt of his pistol, Mendelsohn knocked out enough of the glass sprinters so that the driver could see. Icy cold air streamed in through the hole. Mendelsohn didn't notice. He was sweating heavily with tension and fear.

Someone started to blaze away with a Schmeisser from the nearside ditch. Mendelsohn fired. The man reeled back screaming.

A tyre blew out. The Gestapo man cursed and caught the car just in time. The speed slackened. They could now hear the roar of a motorcycle coming up the road behind them. Hurd yelled above the racket, "Try to knock him out, Mendelsohn!"

"I'll try to, sir," the Marine yelled back desperately.

Their speed was diminishing quickly. It wasn't just the tyre. "The shitting engine's been hit!" the driver moaned.

Mendelsohn leaned out of the window to his right the best he could and aimed. A motorcycle and side car were gaining on them fast with a dark shape poised behind the machine gun set up on the side car. It burst into fire. Someone, or so Mendelsohn thought, screamed with pain at the back of the car. But Mendelsohn was too preoccupied to take in more. He fired. The man on the motorcycle threw up his arms. The combination went out of control immediately. It skidded to a stop in the drainage ditch. Next instant it burst into oil-tinged flames.

Mendelsohn sobbed with relief as the battered Mercedes

spluttered and coughed, losing speed all the time, while the driver changed down frantically in an attempt to keep the car going. But now behind them the firing was dying away and Mendelsohn had the feeling that they were in no man's land between the two enemy lines. Would they, however, make it to the Yanks?

As if in answer to his unspoken question, there was an obscene plonk followed a moment later by the sinister howl of a mortar bomb falling out of the night sky. The battered car rocked violently as the bomb exploded in the field only yards away. "Great crap on the Christmas Tree!" the driver exploded, sweat dripping down his scarlet face. "Now they're frigging well—" His words were drowned by yet another bomb exploding to their right.

"They're zeroing in on us," Mendelsohn yelled. "Stop the car. Let's get the hell out of here before it's too late!"

But it was already too late. The third bomb caught the car squarely on the bonnet. It bucked like a young horse being put to the saddle for the first time. The wheels burst. Next moment it exploded . . .

Cautiously the little American patrol, weapons at the ready, approached the wrecked car, smoke still filtering from its wrecked engine. Up ahead a smoke screen to cover them was being formed by the same mortar team which had knocked out the Mercedes the night before. The smoke was rising quickly in the still grey dawn sky and hiding them from the German line.

The sergeant in charge said, "OK, guys, I go first. Keep me covered." While the others crouched weapons levelled suspiciously, the big NCO advanced at a half crouch, carbine at the ready. He circled the vehicle once, then indicated that the rest of the patrol should advance, while he stared at the interior in obvious bewilderment. "What in Sam Hill's name d'ya make o' that?" he asked no one in particular.

"Christ on a crutch," a PFC exclaimed and whistled softly. "Two dead Krauts, two Nips and a Nip woman. Holy shit, what's going on?"

A little awed the hardened infantrymen stared at the dead bodies piled together in the wrecked car, each man wondering why this strange bunch and the wounded British officer had tried to reach the American lines. Then 'Black Jack' Hawkins, the toughest man in the company said, "Sarge, that Nip's got gold teeth. Have we got time to pull 'em out? I've got my pliers. Fetch a nice price on the black market."

The NCO shook his head. "Ner, the Krauts'll start firing as soon as the smoke lifts. Leave 'em to the niggers of the Graves Registration. They're welcome to the stiffs. Come on."

They slunk away the same way they had come, leaving the corpses to stiffen in the dawn cold. The second SBS mission to Lorient had failed.

Part Four

BREAKOUT

Chapter One

They had marched all night, fifty-five minutes on the move, five minutes resting. The going was hard over the frozen countryside, but there were no complaints. They all knew they were within hours of their objective. "Home to mother," von Dodenburg had explained as soon as they abandoned the V-Mail Express with its precious secrets of the atomic bomb, which would never reach Japan now.

Schulze, whose job it had been to chase away the postal clerks (they hadn't objected much; they were only too relieved to go) and have one last feel at the coloured woman, had snorted, "Right you are, sir. Sell the pig and buy me out. I've had enough of this frog lark." A sentiment with which all the Wotan troopers had agreed.

Now this dawn they were moving through typical Breton landscapes, stark and hard, dominated by craggy-faced stone monuments to the mysterious ancient Celtic people who had once inhabited this remote country. Above them, as they toiled ever westwards, the sky was leaden and ominous, heavy with the promise of fresh snow.

Von Dodenburg felt he wouldn't object if it did snow. It would keep the peasants confined to their houses and, if there were American troops or Maquis in this area, they, too, wouldn't venture out unless forced to.

By the time they reached Quimperle, some ten kilometres from their objective and the sea, it was snowing hard. Their front was almost a white-out and the icy flakes of snow struck their wind-reddened faces like a thousand sharp-bladed stilettoes. Relentlessly the snow poured down and the men marched with it up to their ankles, gasping and panting like ancient asthmatics in the throes of an attack, as they struggled bent-bodied to the coast.

Schulze, bringing up the rear of the column, carried the rifles of half a dozen men who would have fallen out under the strain otherwise, while next to him von Dodenburg supported a young trooper who kept gasping, "Just let go of me, *Obersturm*. Please. I'm holding you up, sir."

Grimly von Dodenburg pressed on against that fearsome weather. All the same he knew he had to find cover for the men soon, even if it was for an hour or two. They had to have something warm to eat and rest.

At four that terrible afternoon, with the light virtually gone and the snow still falling from the heavens as if it would never stop again, Zander who was leading the column plodded back to where Schulze and von Dodenburg struggled, to pant, "Farmhouse ahead . . . fifty metres or so . . ." He wiped the dewdrop off the end of his frozen red snow. "Got to get the men under cover . . . No use going on, Kuno."

Weakly von Dodenburg nodded his head. "Agreed. They're about at the end of their tether, Heinz."

In extended order, the fittest of the exhausted Wotan troopers approached the farm, weapons held at the ready, blinking their eyes constantly to clear their sight of the snowflakes. Zander, who was leading the little force, peered with his good eye through the almost solid white wall in front of him, through which he glimpsed the farmhouse at intervals and spotted the smoke. The place *was* occupied. At least that meant food. But it might mean danger, too.

They came closer. Zander said to Schulze, "Let the two of us go forward and have a look-see." With his hand he indicated the others should halt.

Noiselessly the two of them crept closer through the deep snow, the howl of the storm deadening any sound they might have made. Now they could smell something cooking, but the odour was strange to them, sharp, pungent, peppery. All the same Schulze licked his lips hungrily and whispered, "Some kind of frog fodder, I suppose, sir. Still it's warm and it's fodder."

Zander said nothing. Instead he peered in through the cracked little window of the farm. Schulze looked over his shoulder and gasped. The place was packed with men in ragged *Wehrmacht* uniforms, but some were wearing what he took to be towels over their heads and a few of them were staggering about the place drinking from square-shaped blue bottles, giggling furiously.

"Well, I'll piss in me boot!" Schulze exclaimed. "It's our lot, but they've all got a tan – *in this weather!*" He wrinkled his nose up. Now he smelled something else beside the pungent odour of cooking food. "Holy strawsack, *Standartenführer!*" he exclaimed. "It stinks like a frigging hospital in there. What the frig's going on?"

Zander laughed inspite of the tension, a plan forming almost instantly in his agile mind. "That's ether you can smell."

"Ether. Don't that send you off yer rocking horse, sir?"

"Well, their religion doesn't allow them to drink alcohol, so they drink ether."

"Sir, I think yer'll have to send for the blokes in the white coats with the little rubber hammers." He shook his head. "I don't think I've got all me cups in me cupboard anymore."

"You're not mad, Schulze," Zander said, keeping his eyes on the soldiers inside the big farmhouse kitchen waiting for the huge cauldron over the open fire to boil. "Those are Indians, Indians who were fighting for us."

"*Indians!*" Schulze exclaimed incredulously. "Indians fighting for us. First it's Japs fighting for the *Amis*. Now this. The war's got completely out of hand."

"Yes, look at the one with the turban nearest the window."

"Yer mean the towel head, sir?"

"Yes, see the insignia on his arm? The springing tiger and the legend '*Freies Indien*'*. That means he's a member of the Indian Legion set up in 1942 and recruited from POWs from the Indian Army, we'd captured in Africa. When they came to France there were 3,000 of them. I suspect this lot are deserters or something like that, living off the local countryside."

It took Schulze some time to take in the information, but finally he asked, "What are we going to do with them, sir? The men need warmth and hot fodder. Otherwise a few of them will have to be planted soon to look at the taties from beneath."

"I know, I know, Schulze," Zander allowed himself a wintry smile. "I think we are going to rescue them. You see I think our dear Indian comrades are going

* "Free India". *Transl.*

172

to provide us with the cannonfodder we need once we attack the Tommy base."

Schulze shook his head, even more mystified. "If you say so, sir."

"All right," Zander commanded, "lower your weapon, Schulze, you big rogue. We don't want to frighten them. We're going in." Then to Schulze's even greater astonishment, Zander actually knocked on the kitchen door before entering and saying, "*Jal Hind.*" Whatever that meant.

The Indians, those who were not too intoxicated with the ether, turned in surprise as the cry of the Indian Legion rang out in this remote farmhouse in the wilds of France. Zander pretended not to notice their surprise. Instead he snapped, "*Standartenführer* Zander of SS Wotan, I have been sent personally by Chandra Bose* to rescue you, comrades."

There was a gasp of awed surprise from the deserters.

Again Zander appeared not to notice. "Who is the senior man here?" he barked out the words as if it were perfectly natural to address a bunch of drunken Indian deserters in this manner.

Schulze shook his head in mock wonder.

A small man with glasses who had been warming his bare feet at the roaring fire rose from his chair. "I am he," he said pedantically in correct German and adjusted his glasses to scrutinize these two giant strangers from the SS, who had appeared so unexpectedly out of the snow storm.

Zander said, "You will ensure that my men are fed and warmed, *Herr Leutnant*. We shall spend two hours here at the most. We begin our mission at dusk."

* Head of the renegade Indian freedom movement.

The little Indian looked worried, but he nodded his head, saying, "*Standartenführer*, it will be done immediately." He hesitated, while the others who perhaps didn't understand German looked at him in bewilderment. "But is it permitted to ask how you will – er – rescue us? And what nature is our mission?"

Zander blustered airily, "All taken care of. Discuss plans later when the men are fed." He turned and winked with his one good eye at Schulze. "*Oberscharführer*, order the men inside at once. These good chaps, our dear comrades from India will provide all the men will need, I have no doubt of that."

Behind his back the little officer with glasses rapped out an order.

"*Jawohl Standartenfuhrer*," Schulze bellowed back as if he was on parade, his nostrils assailed yet again by the sharp spice the Indians were using in their cooking, "*Wirds gemacht.*"

He stamped out officiously, while Zander turned and beamed at the Indians who were now hiding their ether bottles and were busying themselves at the fire, chattering excitedly among themselves, perhaps about the supposed rescue, Zander told himself. Not that he cared much what they were talking about. They were double turncoats. Originally they had betrayed their English masters; then it had been the turn of their new German ones. He sniffed. People like that deserved only one thing in the end – the noose or the bullet.

Outside, as the Wotan troops streamed forward through the snow, their weariness forgotten now at the thought of warmth and food, Schulze said darkly to his old running Matz, "Stinks like a pox doctor's parlour in there, it does. Don't think I fancy anything they've touched with their dirty flippers, a frigging lot of towel heads, that's what they frigging are."

"But what's old Zander up to?" Matz asked, as he wiped wet snowflakes off his wizened face for the umpteenth time.

"Search me, old house," Schulze answered. "But I bet my bottom dollar it ain't no good – *for them darkies*." With that he pushed his way through the crowd at the door, crying. "Make way for a senior officer," and entered.

Chapter Two

Fleming said, "I'm scrambling, sir. *Now*." He pressed the red switch and started immediately. "Sir, let me report what I have. Now we have proof that the Germans were – are – trying to get through to Lorient. We found a train they had stolen burned out and virtually destroyed some twenty miles from here. We've also have a message from the US authorities that several of the Americans – postal workers apparently – have turned up and confirmed that the Germans, were in the SS, but dressed in US uniforms. They said they – as the Yanks put it in their quaint way – the Germans had hijacked the train in Eastern France."

Godfrey didn't say anything for a moment and Fleming looked out of the window at the little harbour where the steamer lay, its deck and superstructure white and gleaming with the afternoon's snow. The sailors were busy with shovels getting rid of it over the side. "What of the Jap sub?" the Admiral, back in London at the Admiralty, said.

"Bad news there, sir," Fleming answered.

"What?"

"Poor Harry Hurd bought it with several others of his team. They'd gone into Lorient a second time. But they didn't make it."

"Sorry to hear that, Ian." Admiral Godfrey's gruff tone softened. "Knew his father. He'll take it badly."

"And that's why I'm calling you, sir," Fleming said after a moment, his voice suddenly very urgent.

"Yes?"

"On that stolen train there was an SS general. One of the clerks understood German and twice he heard the – er – hijackers address an older officer as '*Standartenführer*'."

"And what's that supposed to be when it's at home, Ian? I wish you wouldn't be so oblique."

"Price we pay for being in Intelligence, sir," Fleming said with a chuckle which he quickly suppressed, when he heard the sudden heavy breathing at the other end. "*Standartenführer* is an SS general."

"So?"

"Would the Huns risk an SS general on some dangerous mission like this without it being very important. I don't think so, sir."

"I see your point, Ian," the Admiral said thoughtfully. "So what's the drill?"

"I'd like you, sir, to convince the Admiralty to launch an immediate attack on Lorient in order to destroy that Jap sub before it can sail. I don't know, but I've got a funny feeling in my bones that the Jap sub is involved in something very unpleasant for us and the Yanks. It has to be taken out – the sooner the better."

"You have too much imagination, Ian," the Admiral at the other end chided him. "I've always said so. You really should be writing penny dreadfuls. You know that Air has failed time and time again to bomb the Lorient sub pens. The concrete is simply just too thick. Waste of good planes."

"Not by air, sir. But by land."

"*What?*"

"Yessir," Fleming said firmly. "Like we did at St Nazaire in '41 when the commandos went in and blew up the locks etc."

"But dammit, Ian, that would take up too many precious resources," Admiral Godfrey protested. "And we're already scraping the barrel in the UK. Their Lordships of the Admiralty wouldn't buy that."

"They *have* to, sir. It's vital."

"But you have so few hard facts, Ian, but a lot of supposition. They are hard-headed men, their Lordships. What would they make of you a wavy-navy office,* telling them all this stuff? Honestly, Ian, and I must admit I think you really have got something, I just don't think they'd buy it, not from me at least."

Fleming controlled himself with difficulty. Outwardly he had always been the cool, reserved old-Etonian, but inwardly the fires often raged when things didn't go the way he wanted them to. Now, as ever, he was impatient for results. "Then, sir, let me try. I could take the night plane from the US airfield at Rennes and be in London by dawn. Please, sir." For a moment Fleming felt like some pleading little schoolboy, but the matter was too urgent to worry about false pride.

"All right then, Ian. Be it on your own head. I'll fix up a ten o'clock meeting with the naval Chief-of-Ops. See what he says. In the meantime get those SBS people over there to find out all the details of the Hun minefields in the estuary leading up to Lorient. But I warn you, Ian. You must be reasonable and rational about this matter

---

* Royal Naval Reserve, called thus because of their wavy stripes instead of the straight ones of the regulars. *Transl.*

when you meet the Chief-of-Ops, or else . . . "He left the rest of his threat unsaid.

Ian Fleming was not concerned. He said, "I'll take care of the matter, sir. Thank you. I shall see you tomorrow."

Hurriedly Fleming had the remaining SBS teams summoned by Lieutenant Dawes who had now taken over the base after Captain Hurd's death. He told them what he knew or thought he knew and what Admiral Godfrey had asked him to do. "Can you do it, Dawes, with this number of men?" he asked simply when he was finished with his briefing.

"I think so, sir," Dawes, who looked to Fleming as if he couldn't be a day over eighteen, answered. "If that Jap sub is going to run out soon, the German minesweepers will be out clearing a channel for it. We can take it in turns to lie up and watch where the channel is cleared. Then we'll put down buoys to make it easier for our people," he hesitated and looked at Fleming, as if he were afraid he might offend him, "*if* they come."

"They will," Fleming said, face set and determined. It was then that he had his brilliant idea which would get him his 'mention in dispatches'. "Well, when the Germans have cleared a channel, why don't you and your chaps sow a couple of our mines in the centre of that channel near the exit – just in case." He smiled cunningly at the other officer.

Dawes' boyish face lit up. "Wizard idea, sir. It can be done. I'll send the first team out tonight."

"Good, my guess is, Dawes, that nothing will move until those missing SS reach Lorient, if they ever do. After all, they've got to get through the Yanks' lines at Lorient." Fleming looked around at their tough young faces. England ought to be proud that she possessed brave young men like them, who were prepared to sacrifice their lives on dangerous missions for a handful of shillings. He stood up and shook Dawes' hand. May I borrow the jeep to get to Rennes Field?"

"Of course, sir. Will you drive it yourself? I need every man I can lay my hands on for this job. We can pick it up later."

Fleming took one last look at them, then he went to his own quarters to fetch his things while they made preparations for what was to come, a handful of young men who would be dead before the day was out . . .

Matz and Schulze tethered the two horses from the Indians' farm and ploughed through the deep snow of the height above the little port. They knelt cautiously behind a snow-heavy bush and stared down at the place, a huddle of small cottages around a jetty, with further up the road a larger building, outside which was parked a car. "All right, bird brain," Schulze said, "get yer paper and pencil out and start making the sketch for the Old Man."

"My hands are frigging cold. Why always me, eh?"

"Cos I'm a sergeant and you're a frigging lowly corporal. Rank hath its privileges, yer know." Muttering to himself Matz got out his paper and pencil, and with fingers that were red and stiff began making a rough sketch of the little port, which Zander and von Dodenburg would need to plan their attack. At his side, Schulze, who was surveying the little fishing port through von Dodenburg's binoculars, said, "The radio shack's outside the big building where the Tommies are. Get that in."

"All right, all right. I can't go that fast," Matz objected.

"Why don't yer stick a broom up my arse and I'll sweep the snow away as well while I'm doing this?"

Schulze ignored the suggestion, as he swept the line of little cottages with his glasses carefully. There were fishermen's nets hanging up on tall poles outside each of them and he guessed there'd be no soldiers in them, just fisherfolk. "Put those cottages in. We'll have to pass them to get to the boat." He raised his glasses and focused on the little coastal steamer in the harbour. Merchant seamen were busy on her deck clearing the snow away, but he could see no sign of any heavier armament than the twin machine guns just behind the shabby rusting bridge.

"Make a note Matzi, that the crew of the steamer are civvies and there's only a twin machine gun on deck behind the bridge."

"Yes, yes," Matz said, scribbling furiously. "How do you spell bridge?"

"Go and piss in yer—" Schulze stopped short suddenly. The lone jeep was crawling up the snowbound road out of the village, heading straight for their hiding place. "A Tommy's coming," he hissed urgently. "Watch it."

Matz stowed away his sketch carefully and picked up his Schmeisser. Hurriedly Schulze did the same, clicking off the safety catch.

"If he spots us," Schulze said softly, not taking his gaze off the slow-moving jeep for one moment, "let him have it. Then we'll do a quick bunk."

Matz nodded his understanding.

Now the jeep, driven by man in a duffle coat with what looked like a naval officer's white cap set at a jaunty angle, was twenty metres away from the bush where the two of them were hiding. Schulze could see every detail of the driver's face quite clearly, including the long broken nose, with out of the side of the tough-looking jaw, an ivory cigarette holder protruding.

Ten metres. Now he was almost parallel with them. Schulze licked his cracked lips. They didn't want trouble just now. But they daren't risk letting the man get away if he spotted them. He tightened his grip on his trigger.

Suddenly the man started to turn his head in their direction. Schulze took first pressure. The man's head was encircled by his foresight. He couldn't miss at this range. Abruptly the jeep's front wheels hit a deeper patch of snow. The man appeared to curse. His head shot round as the wheels started to spin. With a grunt and another curse he regained control of the jeep and then the jeep was past them and Matz was saying, "That was one very lucky Tommy, old house."

Schulze nodded his agreement.

Thus the future creator of James Bond 007 lived to write Admiral Godfrey's 'penny dreadfuls' after all . . .

Chapter Three

In single file they came down from the hill. It was growing dark rapidly, but the blackout in the fishing village was not too good and there were chinks of light everywhere to guide them to their objective; and out in the harbour, the little coasters was displaying its riding lights quite clearly. Obviously the war seemed now to have passed Port Aven by.

Up front with Zander and von Dodenburg, the little Indian *Leutenant* Patel, was panting already and von Dodenburg told himself the leaders of the Indian renegades was not a very good soldier. Still he had nearly a hundred men under his command to deal with a handful of Tommies; and surprise was on the Indians' side. The Tommies had posted no sentries, as Schulze had reported.

Just before they had set off on the approach march, Zander had warned Patel, "It's vital that you knock out the radio station first. We don't want the English to make contact with the outer world. We'll see the coaster's radio is knocked out as well. Clear?"

"*Klar, Standartenführer*," Patel had answered a little uncertainly, blinking behind his horn-rimmed glasses.

"Then get in that house where the Tommies are billeted and show no mercy. Not one of them must escape."

For the first time some animation appeared on Patel's

dark face and his eyes sparkled. "Don't worry about that, sir. My men have a score to pay back. Not only have they and their forefathers been oppressed by the English colonialists for two hundred years, then when they went to fight for them they were abandoned by their white officers back in '42 at Tobruk."

Zander wasn't in the least bit interested, but he made a polite comment, before taking Patel to one side so that his soldiers couldn't see. He opened one of Grimm's little leather bags they had taken from the train before they had set it alight. He had taken a large gem from the pouch and held up in front of Patel's face. The latter's eyes had lit up greedily. "This is yours, *Herr Leutnant*. There will be several more like it once you have concluded your mission."

"Thank you, sir. Thank you, sir," Patel had replied, holding his hands in front of his skinny chest in a strange gesture almost as if he were saying his prayers, von Dodenburg couldn't help thinking.

"There is one other thing, Patel," Zanier had added, lowering his voice.

"Yessir?"

"Your men will naturally he returned to duty once we reach the safety of the *Reich*. Mr Chandra Bose, however, has other plans for you. You are to return to India on some sort of secret mission."

Patel could hardly contain his delight. "India again!" he exclaimed. "My beloved country again after four years' absence. What delight! Thank you, sir. Thank you!"

Von Dodenburg, watching the two of them, could almost hear the little wheels clicking inside the Indian officer's head as he worked out his scheme. The gems from the Germans would make him a wealthy man. Once the Germans returned him to his native country on this absurd "secret mission", he would quietly drop out, return to his native village and live the good life away from all this misery and slaughter of the war.

Afterwards when they had been alone again, von Dodenburg had said to Zander, "You certainly know to motivate and manipulate people, Heinz."

Zander had grinned and answered, "That's how you become a general, my dearboy. Talk other people into doing your dirty work for you, while you live to die in bed. Come on."

Now they approached the edge of the village. Somewhere a dog had begun barking hysterically. But no one seemed to be taking any notice of it. There was a smell of cooking and von Dodenburg reasoned the fisherfolk would be having their evening meal and wouldn't be bothered with dogs. He hoped so.

They stopped besides a rundown outhouse that smelled of stale fish. Zander turned to a weary and panting Patel. "*Herr Leutnant*, now it's up to you. No one must escape – remember."

"I shall see it to it, sir." Surprisingly enough Patel clicked to attention and saluted.

Casually Zander returned the greeting, and then the two groups parted, the Indians filing past the SS troopers, dark faces set and intent, as they spread out on both flanks heading first for the radio shack.

Zander watched them disappear into the snowy darkness before saying, "That's the last we'll see of those renegades, I hope. Let's move it, Kuno. The balloon'll be going up soon and by then we want to be on the jetty next to the coaster." They, too, then disappeared in the darkness of the village street, heading for the jetty, the only sound the hysterical yelping of the frightened dog . . .

* * *

The radio operator yawned. He had finished reading the dog-eared copy of the *Lilliput* which somebody had left behind in the shack. As always the genitals of the naked girls, which was the main attraction of the pocket sized magazine had been painted over. "Even Jane in the *Daily Mirror* shows more tit than they do," he said moodily to himself, glancing yet again at his wrist-watch. It was still another half-hour before he came off duty.

He shivered. "It's frigging cold in here," he said. "We ain't had our coal ration for this month. Sodding Froggies. Never can get nuttin' right." Now I need a frigging leak. In this weather. Cor stone the bleeding crows." He rose to his feet and put on his duffle coat.

The only latrine in the area was an unsavoury pit over at the larger building, where the men squatted over holes in the ground, holding on to handles, with the feet slip-proof in little slots. Most of them preferred to go outside to urinate. Now dressed in his duffle coat, collar pulled up about his ears, the radio operator ventured forth.

The cold struck him an almost physical blow in the face. He blinked his eyes in the sudden darkness and sought for his flies. "Ruddy thing might freeze to ice in this weather and fall off—" He stopped short, all thoughts of urination vanishing immediately. There was somebody out there: somebody who was up to no good. Why else should anyone be moving so slowly and stealthily in the freezing cold? He backed against the wall and using the old trick of swinging his gaze from left to right at a low angle peered into the night.

Yes, there they were! A good dozen figures starkly outlined against the blackness – and they were armed! He could see the upraised rifles. Christ, he thought to himself in alarm, it's a jerry raiding party from Lorient.

He knew that sometimes they sent out such raiding parties for food, information, now and again for fresh women for their brothels. He swallowed hard. *What was he to do?*

After a few moments he pulled himself together, his nostrils assailed by a pungent smell which he could not identify. He dismissed the smell. The strangers, whoever they were, were getting closer. He heard one of them say something in a language which he took to be German. He *had* to act.

First he must signal to the others higher up the slope that trouble was on the way. Then he ought to summon help. How? Then he hadn't. He sneaked back into the radio shack. He picked up the flare pistol which they used to signal the arrival of boats back from a mission. Making as little noise as possible, he smashed one of the window panes facing the main building, letting the light shine through it so that anyone he now alerted would realize that something was wrong. Why else break the blackout?

As an afterthought he crept back to the door and locked it from inside. Now he was ready. He drew a deep breath, knowing instinctively that now the trouble would start.

He went back to the broken window, thrust the ugly bulbous-muzzled pistol through it and pulled the trigger. The flare exploded in a blinding flash of incandescent white light against the wall of the main building. There was an angry shout of alarm. "That's torn it," he cried and flung himself behind the radio. He rapped out the call signal and cried, "*To all on this net, Pont Aven under attack* . . . To all on this net Pont—"

The grenade came hurtling and smashed through the window behind him. The thick blackout curtain held off some of its force. But not all. Some splinters flew lethally into the little room. The radio operator screamed with sudden pain as the piece of razorsharp steel sliced into his bent back. Gamely he tried to continue as the blood flooded his lungs from his shattered back and chest. "*To all . . . on this net . . . Port Aven under attack . . .*" Then he fell forward into a pool of his own blood . . .

As the first ragged firing broke out from the big building, Lt Patel was furious. "Typically English. You can't trust them," he called. Then he remembered the rewards promised him for taking and killing the English and he cried, "*Jal Hind!*"

"*Jal Hind!*" his man yelled back dutifully, but without too much enthusiasm, as they advanced up the slope. Indeed one or two of them were already faltering, going down on one knee as if they preparing for an aimed shot.

Lt. Patel know the signs. He had seen them often enough in the Western Desert just before an infantry attack had started to fizzle out and become a withdrawal, or even a rout. "They have women up there, English women! They shall be yours for rape!" he lied urgently. "There is loot too. The Horsemen of St George." He meant the British golden sovereigns, which all poor Indians coveted. "They will be yours, too. Forward my brave soldiers. *Jal Hind*!"

This time, at the prospect of sex and money, the response was more enthusiastic. The men advanced, firing from the hip as they did so. But although Patel could see from the number of muzzle flashes, there were only a handful of defenders, and his men were taking casualties. Men were falling everywhere, coming to a sudden startled halt and pitching to the ground, while others were throwing away their weapons and were edging backwards.

The respectacled officer made a quick decision. He pushed his way through the skirmish line, roaring at them, "On my brave soldiers! They are weakening already! *Onwards*!" He tugged the German stick grenade from his boot and threw it at the door. It exploded in a flash of angry violet light. It came tumbling down and the way was clear.

His men raced forward triumphantly, yelling *"Jal Hind"*, in the very same instant that the last burst of machine gun fire caught Lt. Patel in the guts and sent him rolling over and over again down the snowy slope, dead before he hit the bottom, the solitary gem falling from his pocket to disappear for ever.

Chapter Four

"*By the Great Whore of Buxtehude where the dogs piss through their ribs!*" Schulze swore. "The frigging towelheads have gone and buggered it up."

"*Schnauze!*" von Dodenburg cried. "Let's get on the ship before they figure out what has happened."

Together they ran along the snow-covered jetty towards the little coaster. On the other side of the little harbour a fierce fire fight had broken out. As they ran, followed by the rest of Wotan, they could see the scarlet stabs of flame shattering the blackout and the salvos of tracer like flights of angry red hornets.

Outnumbered as they were, von Dodenburg told himself grimly as he pelted through the snow, the Tommies were giving a good account of themselves. Obviously they were not going to surrender to the Indians. He nodded his approval as he ran. At least they'd die as men fighting back rather than just being butchered by the Indians.

Now the crew were stirring on the freighter, alerted by the angry snap and crackle of the small arms fight on the hillside. Someone at the bows shouted something in French. The cry was followed immediately by a signal flare hissing into the night sky. It exploded an instant later, bathing everything below in its icy white light. "*Les boches*," the man at the bows yelled in alarm.

Von Dodenburg fired a burst from the hip as he pelted forward. The man at the bows screamed. Next instant he fell over the side and dropped into the water of the harbour with a splash.

"Shit!" Schulze cursed. "Now the clock really is in the pisspot." Behind the bridge, a dark figure had swung himself behind the twin machine guns.

"*Hit the dirt!*" von Dodenburg yelled and flung himself over the ship's railing followed by a panting Schulze in the same moment that the sailor behind the twin machine guns opened fire. A vicious burst scythed the snowbound jetty. Those troopers who were too slow to obey von Dodenburg's order were bowled over like ninepins, arms and legs flailing in their dying agony.

For a moment or two, while the men on the jetty started to return the fire of those deadly machine guns, von Dodenburg and Schulze lay full length on the wet deck, panting hard and wondering what to do next.

Schulze said, "We can perhaps outflank him, sir, if we swing underneath that lifeboat to the right. That's dead ground."

"How do you mean – *swing*?"

"Over the side. There's a rope hanging there for some reason," Schulze answered.

Von Dodenburg thought for a moment. "All right, try your best, you big rogue. But watch your back. I'm going to tackle the radio room. We must prevent them sending a message—" His words were drowned by a salvo of slugs which chipped the metal all around them. They had been spotted. "Move, Schulze, this place is getting too hot for us."

Schulze moved.

On the jetty, Zander, lying in the snow next to Matz, groaned and shouted above the din, "Matz, we've got to get the men advancing again. Every minute is precious."

Matz bit his lip desperately. He knew what the one-eyed SS General meant. Sooner or later fresh enemy troops would appear on the scene, alerted by the firing or by any message the Tommy radio operators had managed to get off. "Sir, let's try the Wotan rallying cry. Some of the troopers are going to buy it. But not all."

"The Wotan rallying cry?"

"Yessir." Despite the desperate situation Matz gave a little chuckle. "Follow me, men, the general's got a hole in his arse."

Now it was Zander's turn to chuckle. "And so the general has indeed. Matz we'll try it." As if he didn't notice the angry tracer slicing the air, perhaps a metre above the jetty, Zander rose to his feet. "All right, Wotan," he yelled above the racket, "follow me – *the general's got a hole in his arse!*"

"*The general's got a hole in his arse!*" a great bass roar came from half a hundred throats, as the men rose and started pressing forward, bodies bent as if they were advancing against a tremendous wind, firing as they moved forward.

Almost immediately they started taking casualties as the man at the twin machine guns directed his fire at them. But still the survivors kept on, running after Zander who seemed to bear a charmed life. They reached the bows. A sailor popped up, rifle at his shoulder, ready to fire. "Try this on for size, arsehole," Matz snarled and fired from the hip. The sailor fell screaming to the deck, what had once been his face dripping down on to his chest like-red sealing wax.

Now they were clambering over the side, leaving the

jetty behind them littered with the dead and dying. A sailor, cursing furiously, rushed Zander with a club. Zander kicked him calmly in the crotch. He reeled back, his false teeth bulging stupidly from his gaping mouth, clutching his battered testicles.

The machine gunner lowered his sights, swinging the twin guns from side to side. They went to ground again. The fire was too intense. "Heaven, arse and cloudburst," Zander cursed. "Can't we get rid of that swine? He's holding up the whole attack." He gasped abruptly as the slug hit him. It felt as if someone had just thrust a red hot poker into his body. He bit his bottom lip to prevent himself from crying out loud till the blood flooded his mouth. Suddenly he realized he had been hit bad. This was it . . .

Twenty metres away, Schulze moving quickly and very quietly for such a huge man, clambered over the side once more. Now he was parallel and just below the machine gunner on his perch behind the bridge. He crouched there, breathing hard, and looked upwards. He could make out the machine gunner quite clearly. Now, however, for the first time he saw that he had a mate, who was lying full length on the deck feeding the ammunition belt into the gun.

He glanced at the bridge, its windows shattered by gunfire. If there was anyone in there crouched behind the wheel, he couldn't see them. So he had two men to tackle, and he guessed he had surprise on his side. He took a deep breath and seized hold of the rail of the steps which led up to the little bridge cradle.

Not far away von Dodenburg caught the radio operator, as he crouched over his set, twiddling with his dials with one hand, the other pressed to his earphones so that he could hear better. Von Dodenburg grinned evilly. The man wouldn't have been able to hear him even if he were wearing hobnails instead of the rubber-soled GI shoes he had on.

His grin vanished and he concentrated on the task at hand. He knew something about radio-telegraphy, but basically his knowledge was of tank radios. He *did* know that there were automatic signals which worked independently of an operator. He shot a swift glance around the tight little radio room. But he could see no other lights functioning save the one in front of the frantic operator. He guessed that was it.

Now he wasted no more time. He unslung his machine pistol and jammed it into the operator's back – *hard*. The man actually jumped. He swung half round but was stopped by the leads of his earphones. Von Dodenburg jerked them off and with his free hand switched off the control switch. "What nationality are you?" he demanded of the ashen-faced operator, who was staring up at him, as if he were a creature from another world, which in a way he was: an alien from the battlefields of a dozen countries over three continents.

"*Moi, je suis Belge,*" the operator quavered.

That pleased von Dodenburg. If the ship had been English, it would have been a tougher nut to crack. "*Ou est le capitaine?*"

The operator made the gesture of raising a glass to his mouth. "*Il est zig-zag dans la cabine.*"

Drunk in his cabin, von Dodenburg said to himself. Aloud he said, "Can you contact him from here?"

The man nodded swiftly, as if he would do anything to appease the intruder.

"Then do so," von Dodenburg ordered.

With a hand that shook badly, the operator raised the little phone that was in front of him on the metal desk. "*Monsieur le capitaine*," he called. "*Monsieur le* . . ."

Schulze counted off the seconds to himself, *one* . . . *two* . . . About a metre and a half away from where he crouched, the gunner was still hammering away with his machine guns, swinging them from left to right, while the man lying at his side on the wet platform was feeding belt after belt into the gun's breach, the deck all around littered with spent cartridge cases.

Three! Schulze dived forward. The man on the deck looked up startled. Schulze kicked him in the face. He went out like a light. The gunner reacted immediately. He started to swing the twin guns round. Schulze was quicker. His massive fist like a small steam shovel slammed into the gunner's face.

Shulze heard his nose go and felt his knuckles suddenly flooded with hot blood. The gunner reeled back taking his guns with him. Schulze didn't give him a chance to recover. Lifting the guns as if they were kids' toys, he flung them over the side. They landed in the water with a satisfying splash. The danger was over. The ship was theirs . . .

Five minutes later the captain, a dark unshaven man who was still obviously quite drunk, though the shock of what had happened this night was sobering him up, was on the bridge, saying in the thickly accented German of Belgian's *Ostkantonen*,* "But Mr Officer, you can't take my ship off me just like that!"

* Belgium's three eastern provinces which are German-speaking for the most part. *Transl.*

"Don't talk, *act!*" von Dodenburg snapped, as over the water the fighting around the big house still continued. The Tommies were damned stubborn, he told himself. They were rousing the whole countryside. "Get this ship underway at once."

The drunken skipper looked up at him, saying, "And what if I refuse?"

Von Dodenburg laughed harshly and took out his pistol. He pointed it at the sailor and said, "Can't you guess?"

The skipper said, "I'll get on with it, Mr Officer. I'll get on with it."

"You'd better," von Dodensburg said, and put away the pistol in the same moment that Matz came up and tugged him by the sleeve. "Sir, something bad's happened," he said, wizened face very grim.

"What?"

"It's *Standartenführer* Zander, sir. He's copped one. Sir, I think's dying . . ."

Chapter Five

Zander lay on the captain's bunk in the little cabin with the dirty pictures adorning the rusty walls. The sheet they had draped over his wounded dying body was covered in bright red blood, but Zander was still conscious.

For an hour von Dodenburg and Matz, who had some elementary medical training, had worked on him, as Schulze supervised getting the battered Belgian coaster to sea.

But it had been hopeless. They had managed to get his protruding intestines back inside the cavity, but they had been unable to stop the profuse bleeding. Bandage after bandage had been soaked by his blood immediately they had applied them and in the end they had run out of material.

At first Zander had been in great pain after the shock of being wounded had worn off. They had been unable to find morphia in the ship's pitiful medical chest, but they had discovered plenty of cognac in the captain's cabin. So they had been feeding Zander cognac regularly every few minutes ever since they had sailed.

Now the dying general was weak but quite lucid, almost a little happy as if the alcohol were having an effect. "You see, Kuno," he lectured the younger officer. "People like us believed in the cause . . . that's why we fought our war the way we did . . . In reality, however, the war was fought for the middle class." He tried to smile, but failed lamentedly. "I think they always have been, so that your pot-bellied, harassed clerk could get away from the little woman . . ." He coughed thickly and an alarmed von Dodenburg could see the blood in his mouth; his teeth were scarlet with the stuff.

"*Here*," he said. Hastily he held the dirty cup full of cognac to the dying man's lips.

Gratefully Zander took a sip, gasped whispered, "that's better, Kuno. So your clerk could deck himself out in uniform with medals and go and visit whorehouses where the whores wore fancy underwear and did things for him his wifey wouldn't have dreamed of doing. No Kuno," he said after a moment's gasping, "we fought for an ideal. Not your average German, or Englishman and American for that matter. No, they fought for what they could get out of the war." He coughed again. Hastily von Dodenburg wiped the blood out of his mouth so that he wouldn't choke on it.

"Here, take another sip of fire water," he urged.

Weakly Zander shook his head. "Thank you, Kuno, but I don't think I need any more." Suddenly, startlingly he sat bolt upright, his one eye blazing. "What's *it all been about*?" the choked. Next moment he fell back in the bunk heavily and von Dodenburg didn't need to feel his pulse to know that *Standartenführer* Zander was dead.

Matz crossed himself hastily. "God, that gave me a shock, sir!" he exclaimed.

"Me, too," von Dodenburg admitted.

"I've seen a lot o' men croak it in this war," Matz said, his face abruptly very pale," but never like that. And what did he mean, sir, by what's it all been about?"

Von Dodenburg thought he knew, but he wouldn't tell Matz that.

He had to keep the men's spirits up, make them believe that there was something worth going on for. "He wasn't a bad sort of officer, as generals go," he said to no one in particular. Then he reached out and closed Zander's one eye. That done he pulled the blood-stained blanket over the dead man's head. "We'll bury him when we're well out at sea. All right, Matz, there is nothing more we can do."

Matz eyed the half empty bottle of the captain's cognac. "Do you mind if I take the rest of the firewater, sir?' My chest is aching again." He pulled a face.

"Your greedy guts as well no doubt. Yes, take it. Let's see what's going on."

The coastal steamer was ploughing steadily northwards on the course that von Dodenburg had set for the Belgian skipper before he had gone down again to the dying man. Hugging the coast, she was steaming towards Holland and their own lines at a steady seven knots. There was no other traffic visible and for all von Dodenburg knew they could be the only ship at sea. The thought pleased him and as he came onto the bridge, he nodded to Schulze who was keeping an eye on the now sober captain. "All right, I'll take over. You can go and have a chat with that other rogue, Matz. He's got a little surprise for you, I think. *If you're quick.*"

Firewater!" Schulze exclaimed and disappeared like a shot, crying, "I'll have the eggs off'n him with a blunt razorblade if he's gone and drunk all the sauce!"

Von Dodenburg turned to the skipper who was overseeing the helmsman, a bandage soaked in vinegar around his head to alleviate his hungover headache. "Now listen carefully to me, Herr Giskes. You are completely safe as long as you obey orders, and I think it is in your interest to do so. Because if the enemy gets on to us, it will be your ship, your crew and yourself who will suffer. *Klar?*"

"*Klar*," the skipper echoed miserably.

"Now two things." Von Dodenburg stared sternly at him. "One, I give you my word as a German officer that you and your ship will be at liberty to go as once as we are safe." He reached into his pocket and pulled out one of Grimm's pouches. He opened it to reveal the gems sparkling inside it. "Two, some of these will be yours if you carry out orders and take us to our destination."

The little skipper's eyes sparkled suddenly at the sight and von Dodenburg remembered how only shortly before, poor old Zander had pulled the same trick on *Leutnant* Patel, wherever he was now. "I understand. But you must realize, Mr Officer, that our route is dangerous, very dangerous." He rolled his 'r's' dramatically in the East Belgian way.

"How?"

"Because we cross two main shipping lines bringing supplies and troops to Europe from England and America."

"And where are they?"

"First one we encounter is the Southampton-Cherbourg that the Americans use. Then comes the Folkestone-Ostend route used mainly by the British."

"How are they dangerous exactly, more so than any other crossing to Europe?"

"Because your people have those two routes constantly under attack with E-boats, submarines and aerially laid mines. So," the little Belgian skipper shrugged, "naturally the Anglo-Americans go out of their way to protect them. Minesweepers are at work constantly on those two routes. Aircraft patrol them as well, day and night. And there are always flotillas of motor torpedo boats and destroyers buzzing about looking for trouble. I should say that, at the moment, those two routes are the most crowded with shipping in the world."

Von Dodenburg absorbed the information slowly and then he said, "But they won't suspect your ship, will they? You've got an Allied registration."

"No, not normally," the Belgian agreed. "Unless the news of what happened at Pont Aven has got out. Then someone in authority will be asking what the *SS Leopoldville* is doing off its normal supply route, which is to Weymouth." He looked significantly at the young SS officer, as if to say, 'Well, what do you make of that?'

Von Dodenburg forced a wintry smile though he had never felt less like smiling and answered, "Well, let's hope, Captain, that the news hasn't got out. By the way I suggest you speed up this old tub. The sooner we get to our destination the better." And with that he went.

They reached the Southampton-Cherbourg shipping lane just after dawn. In the grey light, they could see ships everywhere, trailing smoke behind them, as they plodded steadily on their courses. To port and starboard of the lane, there were little coal-burning trawlers and minesweepers darting about, trawling for enemy mines, while overheard four-engined Sunderland flying boats of the RAF droned round and round, obviously searching for German submarines.

Von Dodenburg gave the captain back his binoculars after surveying the scene, saying, "I can see now what you mean, Captain. Very busy indeed. Now what's the drill?"

The little Belgian officer shrugged. "We just have to take our chance."

"But if we're challenged by one of those warships or an aircraft?" von Dodenburg persisted.

"Well, we do possess the current code word signal," the Belgian answered. "But if they ask us our Port of destination . . ." he shrugged and left the rest of the sentence unsaid.

Von Dodenburg understood what he meant, however. He did some quick thinking. "You're a Belgian ship, then you're heading for a Belgian port for a repair or refit. That would be logical, wouldn't it? Let's say Ostend."

The Captain was unconvinced. "Ostend doesn't have any shipyards," he said dourly.

Von Dodenburg said, "Let's hope that anyone who challenges you, doesn't know that."

So they started to cut through the long line of supply ships, most of them dwarfing the little coastal freighter. No one seemed to take any notice of them, though the Wotan troopers tingled whenever they came too close to one of the enemy ships. Once they passed a huge troopship packed with US troops. Again no attention was paid to them. Indeed many of the reinforcements for the front were too busy being sick over the side to even look at the Belgian ship, ploughing steadily northwards.

By ten that grey morning they were finally through the shipping lane and were heading for the Channel and the next danger.

Then it happened. Completely unexpectedly a great lumbering flying boat with the roundels of the RAF on its white painted wings came down slowly above them. The Sunderland was so low that they could see the pale blurs of the crew's faces, as it circled the ship and then came back to have another look.

Von Dodenburg clenched his jaw anxiously. Next to

him Schulze growled, "Now the tick-tock really is in the piss bucket. Look, sir, the flyboy is beginning to signal us."

Von Dodenburg groaned. An Aldis lamp was flashing off and on and even though he was unable to read the morse, von Dodenburg knew instinctively what that signal was. The flyboys, as Schulze called them contemptuously, were wanting to know who they were and what their destination was.

Trying to appear casual, he turned round slowly and said to his troopers who were craning their necks and staring at the big flying boat, "All right, stand by for trouble."

Chapter Six

"*She's coming down!*" the Belgian skipper exclaimed in alarm. "She's not satisfied with our reply. Look!" He pointed at the flying boat as it struck the sea some two hundred metres away and started taxiing towards the freighter. "What are we going to do now, Mr Officer?"

Von Dodenburg did some quick thinking. He gave the sea a quick glance. There wasn't another ship in sight. They might just pull it off. "Stop the ship," he ordered the captain hurriedly. "Make it look as if we're quite harmless folk."

"Is there going to be trouble?" the skipper quavered.

"Yes. For him. Now move it."

Hurriedly the captain clambered back onto the bridge. The telegraph clanked twice and as the Sunderland came to a halt some fifty metres away, the ship did the same.

"Smile – smile your heads off," von Dodenburg ordered, "and keep your weapons low."

"I know where I'd like to put my weapon – right up that flyboy's arse," Schulze growled. All the same he obeyed the order and smiled madly at the plane, where a side port had been opened and a loud hailer had been poked through.

"Who are you?" a harsh metallic voice demanded. "And where are you bound?"

Von Dodenburg flashed a warning look at the skipper.

The latter's prominent Adam's apple flashed up and down his skinny throat nervously, as if it were an express lift. "*SS Leopoldville* bound for Ostend," the skipper yelled back, voice thick with fear.

There was silence for a few moments. Von Dodenburg guessed the man with the loud hailer was checking shipping orders or something of that nature.

Again the metallic voice boomed across the intervening water. "No report of you here," it said.

The skipper lied desperately. "Emergency repair. Having trouble with my boilers."

The flyboy was unimpressed. He called, "Coming across to have a look."

"Stand by," von Dodenburg ordered, smiling madly all the time. "Wait till the boat is pushed out of the plane. Aim for the radio mast and the engines. I'll give the order to fire." Despite the cold sea wind, von Dodenburg could feel the sweat tricking unpleasantly down the small of his back.

A dinghy had now appeared. Two men in thick padded overalls got into it clumsily and began rowing towards the *SS Leopoldville*, now proudly flying a hurriedly run up Belgian flag.

"Wait," von Dodenburg cautioned his tense troopers. "Give 'em another couple of metres."

Now there was a brooding silence, broken only by the lap-lap of the wavelets against the freighter's rusting hull and the creaks and slap of the dinghy's paddles.

"*Now!*" von Dodenburg yelled.

The men needed no urging. They knew their very lives depended upon their eliminating the plane and its crew. A vicious volley erupted from the side of the *Leopoldville*. In the dinghy, one of the airman screamed, threw up his hands, as if appealing to God and dropped over the side.

A series of gleaming metallic holes ran the length of the Sunderland's fuselage abruptly. Madly the gunner spun his turret round to take up the challenge. Too late! A burst shattered the perspex and the gunner slumped, dead or unconscious, over the barrels of his own guns.

Von Dodenburg took careful aim. The aerial severed and came trailing down the side of the battered Sunderland. The engines started, whipping up the water into a wild fury. Not for long. A lucky shot hit the port engine. It stopped dead. Still the pilot attempted to get away. The plane started to move.

"Christ, he's doing a bunk," Matz yelled. "That's not very matey, leaving his comrade in the middle of the drink like that."

"Not frigging likely," Schulze snorted and pressed his trigger. A salvo of slugs shattered the cockpit perspex. Another engine went, trailing thick white smoke behind it. Now the pilot was attempting to fly on two engines.

Von Dodenburg could imagine him, sweating and cursing, red-faced and frightened, trying to get the big plane airborne. And sure enough, the Sunderland did start to rise. Not for long. Suddenly it hit the sea again in a great splash of angry water. Almost immediately it started to sink. Hastily the survivors scrambled out of the fuselage and on to the wings, where the dinghies began to inflate automatically.

The men of Wotan gave a hearty cheer. They had done it. Von Dodenburg bellowed above the cheer, "Stand fast! No more firing. The poor shits are going to have enough on their plates if they are ever to get to land." He nodded to the east, where the sky was beginning to darken rapidly. "Comrades," he said, suddenly feeling terribly relieved, "the sky is hanging full of violins." He used the soldiers' expression for snow.

Schulze breathed out hard. "That was nip and tuck, Matzi. I was almost pissing in my pants."

"Almost," Matz exclaimed. "I *did*!"

But relieved as he was, as the *Leopoldville*'s old engines started up once again, von Dodenburg knew they weren't out of trouble yet. On the horizon, darkening by the minute, there had appeared a sudden plume of black smoke. Whatever the craft was, it seemed to be heading in their direction very rapidly. He bit his bottom lip. Had the flyboys been able to radio out for help after all? He looked at the leaden sky and the grey clouds rolling in from the east and started to pray for snow – and soon . . .

Time passed slowly. The snow refused obstinately to fall and the destroyer, for it was a destroyer (they could tell that from the lean grey shape and the craft's high speed) was bearing down on them fast. Now it had become a race between the snowstorm and the unidentified warship. Which would arrive first? And von Dodenburg knew that their only chance now was to disappear into some sort of white-out in which the destroyer would be unable to find them.

At the railing the men of Wotan stared as if transfixed at the warship and then at the snowstorm rolling their way. "Hell's teeth," Matz cried at the sky, "come on, Lord, piss on us. We need it."

The first salvo ripped the sky apart with a noise like a giant tearing a piece of canvas. Water went cascading into the grey sky two hundred metres away. The Belgian skipper moaned and wrung his hands. "My poor ship . . . oh my poor ship!"

Von Dodenburg ignored him. He knew what the destroyer was doing, as she sped ever closer, a bit between her teeth. She was ranging in. Another moment passed and then came that banshee-like howl as the second shell zipped through the grey sky. It fell in a tremendous fountain of angry white water, a hundred metres to port of the *SS Leopoldville*.

By now the Belgian skipper was actually sobbing, great tears of self-pity running down his skinny unshaven cheeks.

Von Dodenburg swore. They had come through so much since they had entered the High Vosges. Now this at the very last moment. "*Zum Kotzen*,"* he cursed aloud.

"Sir . . . sir." It was Matz.

"What is it?" he yelled impatiently.

"*The flag,* sir," Matz yelled back. "Look at the destroyer's flag!"

"What's up with the frigging thing?" Von Dodenburg flung up the Belgian skipper's glasses, for he knew that Matz had the keenest eyes of the whole of Wotan. "They sabre off me leg," Matz was wont to say, "so God gave me frigging good peepers to make up for it."

Von Dodenburg peered through the binoculars at the lean, hurrying shape of the destroyer, men hurrying back and forth along its death carrying ammunition, readying to board the prize, and gasped. The ship was flying the black and white flag of the German *Kriegsmarine*. "Holy strawsack!" he exclaimed. "It's one of ours!"

Now the two forrard turrets were Swinging round to come level with the SS *Leopoldville*. Instinctively he knew that in a minute they would deliver the ship's death blow. *What was he going to do?* How could he convince the crew of the destroyer that they were Germans? They had no signal flags – nothing.

* Literally "sick making". *Transl.*

208

Then he had it. "Start the tannoy system," he cried above the howl of the wind heralding the storm to come, the roar of the ship's engines, the chatter of the machine guns from the destroyer hurtling towards them.

"What?" the Belgian skipper sobbed.

"*Tannoy on!*" he bellowed. "Dammit it, man. Get the tannoy operating. Quick before it's too frigging late!" He swung round to the puzzled troopers. "No questions," he rasped. *"Eins, zwei, drei. Das Wotan Marschlied."*

They reacted immediately, instinctively. As one they burst into that proud hoarse chant which had accompanied them and all those arrogant blond giants, long dead, across the battlefields of half of Europe, once in the great years of victory, now in the grim years of defeat:

> *"Sound the trumpet*
> *Beat the drum*
> Clear the street
> For the men of WO–TAN."

That familiar boastful chant echoed and re-echoed metallicly across the stretch of water between the destroyer and the Belgian freighter. Von Dodenburg clenched his fists hard till they hurt. Would it work?

"*WO–TAN.*" The name seemed to go on for ever.

Then suddenly, starlingly, the destroyer's forrard guns were elevated to their maximum height. Bunting began to flutter hurriedly along the destroyer's yards. A bass cheer rang out and on the destroyer's bridge, a hoarse, drink-soaked voice yelled over the loud-hailer, "*Welcome home, Wotan . . .*"

ENVOI

"*Silence in the knocking shop!*" Schulze bellowed from the head table. "The formal part of the do is over." He grinned weakly. "Now comes the high jinks." He winked knowingly and looked around the big hall, filled with cigarette smoke and drunken, red-faced, excited Wotan troopers.

Already there were a few 'beer corpses' on the floor. Others slumped with their faces in pools of beer, snoring. The naked trooper who had just been running around with a feather duster up his anus, and flapping his arms, crying drunkenly, "Look at me, I'm a frigging fat Dutch chicken", was now vomiting in a flower vase in the corner. A drunk was hanging from the clothes stand by his braces, snoring softly.

"Corporal Matz," Schulze announced, "will now start the high jinxs by telling a dirty story. Corporal Matz commence."

Swaying slightly, chamberpot full of Dutch beer in his right hand, Matz rose. He belched.

Schulze looked at him threateningly. "Watch yer frigging manners, you aspagarus Tarzan."

At the back of the hall at table to himself, von Dodenburg grinned. The diamonds he had shelled out the night before in Rotterdamn's red light district had paid the way for a splendid feast for his men. Now everything was running true to form, the usual Wotan smoker. But this might be their very last. Tomorrow they were being shipped back to the Reich to be refitted for the coming offensive in the West. How many of the excited young men here tonight would survive? Their lives were short and brutish; they deserved what little pleasures they could find.

"Well," Matz was saying, "you know the second thing a soldier does when he comes home on leave to his little wifey?" He grinned drunkenly at his audience and took another hefty swig of good Amstel beer from the stolen chamberpot.

Schulze clapped his big paw to his head in mock pain and muttered, "Oh, no!"

The audience didn't mind. They roared, "What is the second thing a soldier does when he comes home on leave to his little wifey?"

"Why," Matz bellowed. "*He takes off his frigging pack*!"

He sat down abruptly, as the hall exploded in raucous laughter.

Schulze rose to his feet again and glared at Matz. "Why you arse-with-ears, that one's got more white hairs on it than Father Christmas's balls."

"Now, I'll tell a joke – *a real one*! It's about the soldier who had his dick shot off and the pavement pounder in Berlin . . ."

Slowly von Dodenburg finished his *genever*, knowing that it was soon time for him to go. He didn't want to inhibit the men when the whores came, which would be soon. He could already hear the drunken giggling outside as they assembled for what the head whore had called the 'grand finale'.

For a few moments he forgot his surroundings. His

mind wandered back over the events of the last few weeks. The Nisei charging into rifle crying bravely, "banzai", dying for a country which imprisoned their families; big statesque 'Butterfly' who wouldn't go under any man and who had obviously set them up at the pass poor old Zander and that startling death shriek, "What's it all been about?" What indeed?

At the head table Schulze was finishing his story. "So the whore said, 'I'll tell yer a dirty story then, stick me tongue in yer ear and show yer me tits!" The hall erupted into drunken laughter, followed by catcalls and troopers throwing bread rolls at Schulze. The latter held up his arms for silence with that tremendous, "*Silence in the knocking shop!*" of his.

He waited a moment till the noise had died away, his face purple with drink, the sweat pouring down his broad face, then he said, "*Kameraden*, now to the high point of the evening. The moment you've all been waiting for, 'cept them of you who are warm brothers."* He made a limp wrist gesture.

Again there was laughter and shrill whistles.

"*Les girls!*" He stamped his foot down hard three times.

Outside a high pitched female voice said in Dutch, "*een . . . twee!*" A drum was banged. A trumpet sounded. There was the sudden blare of military brass.

The great doors were flung open. The audience gasped.

Standing there, proud and erect, drum major mace in her hand, clad in a steel helmet and jackboots, but otherwise completely naked, there was a huge imperious-looking woman. Behind her there was a

---

* German slang for homosexuals. *Transl.*

female military band, all naked, too, save for helmet and boots.

"*Wow*!" they gasped. "I'm going to faint," they cried. "I'm coming," others yelled. Men blinked their eyes as if they couldn't believe what they had just seen. Others grabbed wildly at their crotches. At the main table Schulze looked proudly at his great surprise, then nodded his head.

The huge woman raised her mace high above her head so that they could see the tuft of jet black hair underneath and cried in German, "*PARADEMARSCH*!"

With the room trembling in that great blare of brass, the kettle drums rattling, the bass drum thudding away and sounding the cadence, the naked women started to goose-step into the room, raising their legs high like Prussian guardsmen so that nothing was left to the imagination of the awed, delighted troopers of SS Assault Regiment Wotan. The orgy could commence . . .

Outside in the cold winter night, von Dodenburg stared at the icy silver of the unfeeling stars, and listened idly to the muted racket coming from inside, for the naked whores hadn't managed to cross the room before the troopers had attacked them. From the east there came the faint noise of the barrage. It was starting all over. Soon they would be part of that battle over there, von Dodenburg knew that. Suddenly he felt very lonely.

"You like jig-jig, soldier?" a soft voice enquired from a darkened doorway. "I've give you good time."

He spun round. A woman was lounging there. In the faint light she looked young and pretty.

"I'm not expensive," she went on in that nice soft voice. "Twenty cigarettes and ten more as a tip if I please you."

Why not, a little voice at the back of his head prompted. Go on, Kuno, enjoy yourself for once.

Who knows what the morrow will bring.

Von Dodenburg said, "Oh all right. I'd like to very much."

"Good," she said. "Come on, darling." She put her arm through his and he could smell her cheap scent, but her body felt warm and soft. Moments later they had disappeared into the blackout, chatting away merrily, as if they had been friends for life . . .